Overcoming The Battle
"I Know My Identity"

By
Evora Bentley

Printed in the United States of America
10 9 8 7 6 5 4 3 2 1
2nd Edition – August 2017

Tweedy Poole's Publications & Consulting
"Building The Kingdom One Book At A Time"

Overcoming The Battle

"I Know My Identity"

Overcoming The Battle

Dedication

I dedicate this book to my mother
Brenda F. Bolden Bentley
July 14, 1957 - September 2, 2000
God rest her soul, and may she rest in peace

I watched her as a single mother work very hard as she strived to be the best mother, sister, and daughter she could be. She was a light that brightened the room when she walked in, always willing and ready to serve and help people. My mother was so full of love with a memorable smile, quick to make you laugh. I can't remember her complaining when she worked a twelve hour shift and a part time job at a fast food restaurant. As a single mother she did what she had to do to provide for her children.

During her battle with breast cancer, she continued to be a light that shined until her last days here on earth. Because of her I am motivated to strive to live a life full of perseverance and push to accomplish any task God places on my heart.

I saw her as a hard worker, which has motivated me to work even harder to do what others may think is impossible. I am determined to make it possible so that I can instill the same behavior in my children and pass it down to generation after generation. If possible, I only strive to be as good or a better mother, wife, sister, daughter, and friend as she was.

R.I.P. mom, I miss you and cherish every memory of you.

Overcoming The Battle

Acknowledgements

First, I would like to give honor and thanks to my Lord and Savior Jesus Christ. I give God all the glory for the blessing in which I believe this book will be for others. I am thankful to God for the gift of writing as well as other gifts He has placed inside of me. I thank Him for trusting me to use them, and for that He shall receive the Glory. My life changed for the better back in, October 2005 when He came into my life and we started our relationship.

My children Breaunna, Kierra, and Azaria Starks you're my daily motivation to live life to its fullest, to pull out everything God has placed in me so that you will do the same.

Thank you to my pastors & spiritual parents Dr. Stacy and Denae Lemay, of Champion Kingdom Center, in Pineville, N.C. I greatly appreciate you and I'm blessed to receive the Kingdom teachings and growth that I receive weekly. Thank you for being great examples and willing vessels for The Kingdom of God. Your examples have caused my desire for God to burn even more. I am beyond blessed to have the Lemay's being an impact as part of my life's journey.

Tweedy Poole, author, and coach of Tweedy Poole's Publications & Consulting, you have been a great mentor and friend who believed in me. Especially, on those days when I thought about quitting, but you pushed and always encouraged me. I love and thank you for that.

Apostles Ron and Hope Carpenter of Redemption World Outreach Center, in Greenville, SC, thank you so much for the teachings I received when I attended Redemption World Outreach Center. I never understood or believed purpose was placed inside of me until I started receiving your teachings. After each service I felt like I was becoming who God called me to be.

To all my family and friends who encouraged and believed in me to do a great thing, words can't express how much I thank and love you for believing in me.

Giovanna Burgess, I thank you for being such a role model of inspiration. Tammy Foster, thank you for not only being a good personal trainer, but also a great friend who blessed me with encouraging words.

Shanekqua Williams, Ashannon Hughley, and Montina McMorris thank you for believing in me, it means the world to me. Varnessa Bails, my beautiful friend/sister, you have no idea of the inspiration and impact of change you have been in my life. I thank you and love you dearly. A special thank you to my mentor and friend Amadi Blessbe Udoji, thank you for coming alongside and being the midwife, I needed to birth this project, you believed in me more than I believed in myself. By God's grace HE sent you when by sight, it looked like my dreams were dead, but they are very well alive. May God continue to bless you all abundantly.

Winner of My Thoughts

Where did that thought come from?
All these thoughts are running through my mind,
It's like ammunition combined.
I've heard that same thought for years,
It has been embedded in my soul.
Where did it come from?
I do not know?
I can't take this anymore!
I don't want to hear it!
It's destructive to my spirit.
The thought tells me I'm nobody,
But God says I'm mighty!
God says you have a calling on your life.
I want the thoughts to be destroyed.
They are filled with so much strife.
I have to empower myself daily;
I refuse to allow these thoughts to have power over me.
They are a distraction to whom I'm called to be;
But no longer do they deceive me anymore.
Once the thoughts try to enter,
I STOP THEM AT THE DOOR!

Overcoming The Battle

Prelude

I've tried everything, but still couldn't get any sleep. If only I could get two hours. This house is way too quiet; maybe putting on some music will help me, even though I've tried three times already. I wasn't even sure if I wanted to go to sleep or if I just couldn't. I'd been having the same dream all week, *I wondered if it was trying to tell me something?* I know it's not real because I keep calling to check on the children.

My fear was that what happened to me would also happen to them. I don't want it to, but from time to time I think, *'What if it did happen?'* That has been my fear since the day they were born. "Carmen, you have to get a hold of yourself." It was 3:37 a.m., and I had to be at work in less than four hours.

"It is time," I heard the calm voice say. "It's time to let the healing begin. It's time to release."

'I can't, it's been a secret for too long, I don't want to. I'm just going to let it be. There's no need in stirring up the past. As far as I'm concerned it's dead.'

There was that feeling I've tried to shake for the last twenty years. I need something to eat, and then to sleep I'll go. Food always soothes me, but the cookies were no longer on my dresser. I forgot I ate them the other night when I was having a moment.

I couldn't believe there wasn't any junk food to remove the emotions I was feeling. Depression, discouragement, resentment, and worthlessness all started to rise within me. Tears rolled down my face which startled me because my crying days were over. I refused to shed anymore tears; nothing or no one else was going to get my tears.

Visions of incidents recounted in my mind from years ago as I reached for my cell phone and searched the internet for possible effects from past events. I tried to make myself believe or think I had blocked them out, but obviously I hadn't.

There was no surprise that I had found a whole list of categories pertaining to my situation. After reading so many stories I discovered that others were experiencing the same thing I was going through.

While reading, the tears I told not to fall, fell anyways. Why couldn't I make the memories vanish? Wait! What would others think of me? What will they say about me? They'll think I'm a liar.

"You seem unaware of how it has affected you," said the calm voice.

It's happening again – I could see all the misguided relationships I'd encountered and how they hurt me. Oh, how I wished I could take a pill and make it disappear. Reaching for my purse, I moved my hand around inside feeling for a cracker, a candy bar, anything. When I turned my purse upside down a card fell onto my bed. I had glanced at it several times before, but never expected to use it.

The card was from a nice lady I had met at Darby's; a local market a few blocks from my house. I stared at it for a moment and this time something prompted me to dial the number. *'Would the number still be the same? I wondered,'* it had been a little over three months since we had met.

"Give the number a call. You'll be glad you did," the voice instructed. "This will be your beginning steps."

That day in Darby's a woman approached me and said, "Hello beautiful lady, God has such a great plan for you."

I looked at her like she was crazy thinking, *'Out of all the people in the store, you decided to approach me?'* Then she reached in her brief case and handed me a card that read, "Singleton's Ministry, Prayer, and Deliverance," 24-hour hotline.

It will be crazy to call and tell my business to a complete stranger. I threw the card back inside my purse and kicked it on the floor. Lying in bed I folded my body in a fetal position and began to cry, shaking and rocking myself back and forth. There was a battle going on in my mind and the negative thoughts were winning. "You're nothing! You're worthless! It's your fault and now you want to sit and cry about it," a strange voice said.

I hated the sound of that particular voice. It always spoke words in a negative tone. Then there was the voice that spoke in a comforting tone. "Those are lies, so don't believe them, you are beautiful. You were created for a unique and special purpose. Even though your life experiences may have been rough, your ashes will become your beauty."

What does that mean; *"my ashes would become my beauty?"* None of the mess I had gone through could be turned around or changed. The voice was a little soothing, but I sat there thinking, *'There's no way that's true. How could it be?'*

The thoughts of not having a purpose or meaning in this world seemed more believable than whatever beauty turning into ashes were. I had gotten use to battling the thoughts all my life, so I didn't expect a different outcome.

After hearing the voices, I got off the bed and picked my purse up off the floor. As I pulled the card out of my purse I was still unsure, but dialed the number anyway. On the third ring I contemplated hanging up, but then a voice said, "Singleton's Prayer Line, God bless you. How can I help you?"

"Um…I guess I want a prayer?" I said, unsure of what I was actually doing.

"Hi, my name is Victoria, what's yours?" Then she paused for a moment and said, "That's only if you want to give it to me."

"My name is Carmen Wilson," I whispered.

"Well hi Carmen, you sound upset, but I know God will give you the comfort you need. What has led you to call tonight, well this morning I should say?"

I couldn't speak, and my crying became uncontrollable. "Everything's going to be alright. God will get all the Glory," Victoria said in a soothing voice.

Before I could say anything, she began to tell me about my life. "How did you know?" I asked.

"Sweetheart, the Holy Spirit knows all things. You must understand that most of the time what we go through in life God will take and use it to help somebody else. You have so much bitterness and hatred in your heart. Allow God to free you and show you what He can do."

"God will get the Glory out of it, but you have to believe and be willing to do the work to release it. You are such a strong woman, and I'm sure you know from experience, *"what doesn't kill you only makes you stronger,"* she continued.

I thought about the sermon I heard two days ago by Pastor Susan Bridges. I had watched her on the internet several times before and was amazed at how God used her to inspire others. I remembered her saying, "Nothing you have gone through in life will ever be a waste, because what you went through was never about you. It's all about how God is going to use you."

It amazed me that Victoria told me exactly what I had heard two days ago. As I told her about the message she said, "Now, see how good God is. He connected you with me, so you could receive confirmation."

As she spoke I continued to cry. "Carmen, go ahead cry, scream, shout, and do whatever is necessary."

"I've done that so many times, I'm tired. I feel like I'm about to lose my mind!"

"Do it some more, it's cleansing your soul. But this time, ask God for healing, and guidance to set you free and this time believe it."

I formed my mouth to do what I had done so many times before hoping for a different outcome. "God, I need your help! I need your guidance. I'm so lost and don't want to be like this!" After screaming, crying, shouting, and asking God for direction in my life, I had to admit I felt much better. Victoria gave me her direct contact information and said to call her anytime.

As I ended the call, I threw my hands up in the air. "Okay God, I'm ready, my heart is open, and I'm willing. Please show me what to do. I know I can't do it without you." This was the beginning of me becoming free from everything that kept me from being the "authentic me."

Chapter One

It was great to finally have a day off. There had been so many phone calls from people ordering the new Universal Jupiter cell phone. It had so many capabilities it was like something from another planet. That's how it got its name. I especially was glad to be off from all the mandatory overtime. I had worked at Dynamics Wireless Company for eight months, and was sick and tired of it.

There were so many days when I wanted to quit in the middle of a phone call. The stress was unbearable at times. It wasn't only the job itself, but the micro-management as well. Our bathroom time was only included in our break. They made us feel like we were in jail. There was not one employee that could get up from their desk without my supervisor standing up from his. He watched them walk to the restroom, asking where they were going. Everybody thought he was crazy.

Today has been an enjoyable "me time," type of day. I thought about calling Henry, my supervisor at the club where I worked in the evenings and telling him I wouldn't be in tonight or I'd be there a little later. At times, Henry acted, as if I was the only one who knew how to work the bar.

My sister Charlotte, was such a big help with the kids, I couldn't have asked for a better baby-sitter. She was also extra generous today. She had called and asked if

Mackenzie and Taylor could spend the night. She still insisted even after I told her I may not be working tonight.

Hopefully my boyfriend Devin will have some good news about a job when I get home. He had lost his job about four months ago and was receiving unemployment. While he looked for a job, he started pawning items to bring in a little extra cash. I didn't like it, but respected the man for wanting to take care of his family.

Relieved that my phone had assigned ring tones, I watched my dad's number flash on the screen and debated answering or letting it go to voicemail. Who was I kidding? I forever wanted a loving father/daughter relationship with him. Unfortunately, we had a love-hate relationship.

Some days I loved him so much, but then there were those days I'd be so mad at him for not being there for us. There were times when we had great conversations, and then the next time we spoke we'd argue non-stop. Here I was twenty-seven years old still believing one day he would be the father my sisters and I always longed for.

Sometimes our arguments were very bad. He would piss me off by saying something stupid, and I'd tell him I hated him, and the argument would flare from there. No one would have ever believed I was speaking to my father if they heard some of our conversations. We had been having those kinds of moments since I was about ten years old.

"Pretty Boy," is the nick name he gave himself, would get mad and tell me I was nothing and would never amount to anything during some of our arguments, and his voice rang loud and clear in my head. "You ain't nothing but a big disappointment, having all them babies out of wedlock."

I always wanted more in life and to be different, but Pretty Boy's words had an impact on me. His harsh words would oftentimes cause me to give up on certain tasks. Our calls normally ended with one of us hanging up on each other, and the following week we'd be back to our regular conversation – it was so weird.

His words were seeds that were planted which I wished had never grown. It would have been great to have the type of father who protected his children and told us we were beautiful instead of us needing to hear it from other men. "Let's see what he has to say today," I sighed before accepting his call. His call irritated me because I was picturing myself in the attire I had purchased to wear for Devin tonight. "Hello," I answered rolling my eyes.

"My angel, how are you doing today?"

"Hi, I'm great Pretty Boy, how are you? I'm not up to much, just leaving the mall."

"How are those beautiful granddaughters of mine?"

"They're fine. Is everything okay?" I asked wanting him to get straight to the point.

"Oh, nothing much, I'm on my way home for a few days."

"I thought you were in Minnesota?" I asked, though I knew he wasn't.

"I was up there working, but that crazy prejudice boss of mine knit picks about every little thing, so I decided to take a few days off. Now I'm exploring my options. There are a few job openings in Florida. It'll be good to be at home with my family. Well, you know the family I have there. It has been different since you and the girls moved away."

Pretty Boy said it would be better if he found employment in Florida to be near my sister Chasity. In his mind everybody was prejudice and against him because he dated outside of his race. I thought it was the silliest thing, especially since everyone had a good reason not to like him. It was usually something he had done, nothing to do with his marriage.

"I know, I do miss Florida sometimes, but things are really great here in Houston. "I never thought Texas would be so interesting, we enjoy living here."

"Okay, well as long as you guys are happy, that's all that matters. But, I'm ready for you to come home and visit. It's been awhile since I've seen y'all."

"Hopefully, we will be able to visit soon."

"I hope so. Hey Carmen, I wanted to ask you a favor."

"What's that?" Here it comes; I knew he wasn't calling me to shoot the breeze.

"See if you can help your daddy out a little?"

I knew it was something – Frederick Wilson, better known as, "Pretty Boy" wasn't calling to see how we were doing. His main priorities when we were young was running women, dressing to impress, while we walked around with holes in our clothes. He never thought about what we ate, and certainly didn't care where we lived. And let's not forget the white powdery drug he kept on the tip of his nose.

Whenever he was high he abused our mother. Now he needs us. Life has a funny way of turning the tables. "Butterball, I want to know if I can borrow $300.00. I was supposed to pay the light bill, but I had to get my car fixed."

"Uh huh…" I was ready to end the call, but patiently listened to his sad sob story.

Butterball is the nickname given to me by my family when I was younger. Why couldn't they have given me a nickname like, Red, which would have been appropriate since I had red hair, or Hazel, because of my eyes? No, they had to pick a name that described my size.

Growing up I was never the skinny girl, so once one family member started calling me Butterball they all jumped on the bandwagon. For years I tried to lose weight, but nothing worked. There must have been a ton of different diets and diet pills which were supposed to have done the trick, but they didn't.

Food had been my best friend for as long as I could remember. It always got me through sad days, bad days, hopeless days – well any day for that matter. I used food to deal with my battles. It seemed to have helped, even if it was just temporarily. At the height of only 5'3", I weighed 190 to 210 lbs. since the 10th grade. After I had my children my weight has been at a steady 250 lbs.

One thing I could appreciate was that my stomach didn't stick out more than my behind. Most of my weight was in the lower parts of my body, butt, legs, and thighs. Some guys called it thick, and others just called me fat. As I got older I learned how to live in the skin I was in.

"Butterball, your mother can't find out I'm struggling to pay the bills, she's just starting to trust me again. I'm trying; you have to believe I am. I've been doing everything I can to get our marriage back on track."

"She's my step-mother, not my mother," I quickly corrected.

It's not that I had anything against my step-mother, but my mother had passed away only three years ago, and I guess I thought it was a little disrespectful calling another woman Mama. I wasn't ready to put another woman in her place.

"Pretty Boy, why don't you just tell her the truth; that you had to get your car fixed?"

Little did he know I had already spoken to his wife. She called the other day crying about him being laid-off and how she couldn't wait until he found a steady job. He lied and said he was laid-off because he was fifteen minutes late dropping off office supplies. He had told her it was the first time he had ever been late, and his boss fired him.

Pretty Boy drove around the country delivering office supplies to business offices. He wasn't fired for arriving fifteen minutes late, and I'm sure it wasn't the first time. Whatever his story was I wasn't going to get in the middle of it.

Nancy Franklin, his wife and my step-mother was from a wealthy family. She owned several dry cleaners that had been in her family for over twenty years in Georgia, North Carolina and Florida. Nancy also owned Franklin's, a five-star steakhouse restaurant and a club in Atlanta, Georgia.

Nancy lived in a stunning three story, five-bedroom house that set on four acres. She even made one of the rooms into a small movie theatre. So, money was not an issue for her, but her husband, well that's a different story.

Nancy's black Mercedes CLK 500 and blue Jaguar XJ were always clean and parked in her three-car garage. I always thought she was too good for Pretty Boy, but she was fifty-five and very gullible. I felt kind of sorry for her; she had no idea what she was getting herself into. After a few dates she said she knew he was the one, so she proposed to him and they were married within a month.

My father really thought "Pretty Boy" was his name. He even had it tattooed on his left arm. When he filled out job applications he would write Pretty Boy in the *name* space. He was a real ladies man; tall, stocky, had natural curly hair, pecan tan, and dark green eyes. He was a real smooth talker that would have a sanctified, Holy Ghost filled, preacher's wife debate if she should go with my dad or stay with the man she exchanged vows with.

Even with all his character flaws, how could I turn my back on him? I guess I thought giving him money would encourage him to start being the father we always needed. I had always told him "yes," regardless of what we went through. "Alright, Pretty Boy, text me your account number and I'll send it to you."

"Well, baby it would be so much better if you could wire me the money."

"Wire the money? That's going to cost almost $30.00. Why can't I deposit it into your bank account?"

"Well right now, it has a negative balance. Somebody broke into my account. I was a victim of identity theft, so I'm in the process of disputing the charges."

'Sure, he was. He was the victim and the one who committed the fraud.' I kept my thoughts to myself.

"Alright, I'll wire it to you in the morning. I'll give you a call when the funds are available."

Pretty Boy could receive an award for the many lies he told. He should have pursued a career as a professional liar. "Thanks so much, I can't tell you how much this means to me."

After I agreed to give him the money he started rambling talking about Uncle Greg. "Nancy is still mad about the time your Uncle Greg came to visit and ordered porn and ran the cable bill up to a $1,000.00. I think she thought I had something to do with it."

Of course, Nancy thought he had something do with it. She couldn't believe anybody could watch that much porn in such a short period of time. Uncle Greg, well, he wasn't really my uncle, but daddy's best-friend. They had been friends since the ninth grade.

I used to love him because he spoiled me rotten. He would buy me whatever I asked for and take me wherever I wanted to go. Even though they weren't blood, you would have thought they were brothers instead of friends.

"Pretty Boy, Charlotte has the girls for the night, so I need to call and check on them. I have to go. Talk to you later. Love you." I said abruptly, snapping back from memory lane

"Okay baby, thanks again, tell your sister I said hello and I love her."

Charlotte only answered Pretty Boy's calls once a month or every other month. "Okay, I sure will," I said hanging up.

As I dialed Charlotte's number I contemplated passing on Pretty Boy's message. She always had something sarcastic to say whenever we talked about him. "Hey Charlotte, I was calling to see how the kids are doing? I can come get them if they're too much trouble."

"Girl, they're fine, please stop calling every five minutes and enjoy your night."

"Alright, thanks Sis, love you. I'll see you tomorrow. Oh yeah, Pretty Boy said to tell you hello and that he loves you."

"You could have kept that message undelivered. Nobody was even thinking about him. I'll see you tomorrow, love you too. We will not be accepting anymore phone calls from you tonight," she laughed.

Charlotte never called me Butterball. She gave me hope that one day I would lose some weight and escape the nickname. My sister sacrificed so much when she moved to help me with the kids. She even dropped out of college and enrolled in the community college when she came to Texas. My sister and I have an unbreakable bond. Charlotte knew my deepest secrets and swore not to tell a soul. She felt sorry for me, cried for me, she even swore to always be there for me, and that's exactly what she's done.

After hanging up with Charlotte, I looked forward to spending a quiet evening with Devin. When I pulled up to our beautiful two-story home, I sat in the driveway amazed at its sight. It was day light savings and the sky was transitioning. The yellow tulips in the flowerbed complimented the burgundy shutters around the windows. It looked like a home featured on the cover of a home gardening magazine. It felt like a fairy tale that had come true. I wouldn't have ever imagined living in such a

beautiful place.

We were so excited when we moved into the house. Devin had a great job and made sure all the bills were paid on time. There were no worries at the moment, but if he didn't get a job soon we may get evicted. Now the bills were my burden to carry.

Our home life was totally different than the housing projects I grew up in Smithstone James. My mother struggled to keep the bills paid. Even though she worked hard we were still poor. I remember eating mayonnaise sandwiches for a week straight because she had to wait until her next pay check to buy sandwich meat.

Our apartment was always filthy; dirty dishes piled high, floor dirty and no one ever took out the trash. Momma worked two jobs and depended on daddy to keep the house clean, but he never did. I was so glad when I got old enough to keep the cleanup. I was sick and tired of the trash and the rats taking over.

There were many nights when we would stay at our grandmother's house while my mom worked sixteen hour shifts. Those were the best times ever. We ate good, slept good and never had to worry about the rats.

Our family members rarely came to visit because of the filthiness of our home. My dad friends were over all the time. They didn't seem to mind the mess as long as they had a place to party. Marijuana, liquor, and beer bottles were all over the place. I guess they didn't mind the mess, since they were the ones making it.

When Chastity was five, she cut her foot on a beer bottle and had to get nineteen stitches. After that he cleaned up a little, but not enough to make a difference. I certainly don't miss those days, or the memories that came with them.

Overcoming The Battle

Chapter Two

"Why are all the lights off?" I wondered walking towards the door. Devin's car was in the driveway, and I know he's not asleep this early. Well, if he is that's about to change. I put the key in the lock, turned the knob and barely entered the house when me and all my items were knocked to the floor. "Devin!!!" I grabbed the side of my face in unbelief.

"Where have you been? You were supposed to be home over an hour ago? I know you been out there with one of your 'lil boyfriends. You a good for nothing whore!" He said smacking me again.

There he was putting his hands on me for the thousandth time. I thought we had gotten past the abuse, but obviously not. "Have you lost your mind? Have you been drinking?!"

As I picked myself up from the floor I looked towards the living room where I saw the unexpected. I rubbed my eyes to make sure my vision was clear. Lines of white powder were on the glass coffee table with a hundred-dollar bill rolled up beside it. "Devin, are you serious?!" I cried. "Cocaine Devin, you've been clean for almost a year. Don't you remember all the hell we went through? Devin, did you for once think about me and the twins?!"

It seemed like the old Devin had slid back in. He was so jealous and insecure. When I would leave the house, he used to check the speedometer to make sure I didn't go over a certain mileage. Devin was always accusing me of cheating.

"Don't be questioning me. Where were you?"

"I went by Savannah's house to see how she was doing? I was only there for twenty minutes."

"I don't know why you're always hanging around that slut."

"Savannah's not a slut!"

"Your friend is a slut, and if you are hanging with her, you a slut too. You should've been home the time you said you would be!"

I was so mad, hurt, and confused coming home to this I was ready to fight. I stood face to face and pulled my arm back with my fist balled ready to punch him in his face, but he grabbed my arm as I swung, "You are so stupid Devin! I'm leaving; I can't do this with you anymore!"

Savannah told me I deserved better. When she found out he was putting his hands on me I had to stop her from putting a hit out on him. Savannah wasn't the type to hold her tongue, so I tried my best to keep them apart. She also told me Devin was keeping such tight reigns on me because he was the one cheating.

As much as I wanted to defend him she was right. He had cheated on me a few times – okay, maybe a few to ten times. I had even been in several fights with some of the females he had been with.

My sisters and I never wanted to be with a man like our father, but somehow or another I ended up falling in love with a "Pretty boy," and I'm not talking about his looks.

When I met Devin, I could hear my mother's voice saying, "What looks good Carmen is not always good for you."

My face stung, but today I had to stand my ground. It was time to go, but Devin's hurtful words hit me like my father's. "You ain't going nowhere! Who's going to want you? Ain't no man trying to take care of you, and you must be crazy if you think you're going to bring another man into my girl's life," he said sucking his teeth.

"Devin, I'm serious, I can't do this anymore. I am so sick and tired of you putting your hands on me and accusing me of being with other men when you are in our home doing drugs. What is wrong with you?! And don't tell me it's about a man."

"Carmen, you act like this happens all the time. This is one little mistake; you know it's been a while since I hit you."

"Devin, you shouldn't be hitting me at all. I will not go back to letting the girl's watch you beat on me."

"Baby, I've been so stressed trying to find a job. It hurts me to see you working so hard to pay the bills. And you know my unemployment check is about to end. I can't take it anymore. I can't take care of my family! Carmen, it makes me feel like less of a man," he said with his head held low.

"I slipped Carmen…I slipped, but you don't have to worry about it happening again," he said grabbing me by the hand.

"Devin, how did you get the money?" I asked pulling my hand away.

There was a pretty good amount of drugs on the table from what I could see. "Carmen, don't worry about it, I got it from a friend," he stuttered.

Immediately, I ran upstairs to our bedroom and looked in the closet for my old purse I hid behind a shoe box. It was no surprise he had found the stash. Why didn't I think of a better place, or opened up another bank account? I had been saving that money for a rainy day. It was the money I made working at the club. I had saved $1,500.00.

I ran back down the stairs as fast as my feet could take me. "Devin, you stole from us!!! There's only $800.00 in here! That was money to help with bills when needed. You are so selfish, always thinking of yourself!" I took the remainder of the money out and threw the purse at him.

"I didn't touch that money to buy drugs. Roderick hooked me up. You know I'm not about to buy that stuff," he said, unable to look me in the face.

Roderick had been Devin's best friend since the sixth grade. It was sad to say that the friend he loved the most was nothing short of a Judas Iscariot. In the past he had stolen money from Devin and even from me, of course he denied it, but everything led to him. "Babe, I'm sorry, I'm sorry. I'll do whatever you want me to. It won't happen again, I promise."

"I've heard that a thousand times." Devin had given me over a thousand promises and broke every last one of them. The only one he had kept was being a great father to his kids. He may have done wrong by me, but he loved our girls.

"I used the drugs, but I didn't touch that money. You have to believe me!"

Devin walked behind me grabbing my arms, and trying to hug me. By that time the sound of his voice had changed. Being the smooth talker he was, he knew just how to calm me down. He placed one hand on top of mine then started rubbing my face with the other as he gave me another, "*I promise to do better,*" speech.

It was over once he started caressing my thigh, telling me how beautiful I was, how much he loved me, and couldn't live without me. I guess I always fell for it because I didn't hear it often. "No, no, no, stop it," I said trying to remove his hand, but it was feeling so good I fell into a trance.

"Carmen, you and the girls are the best thing in my life."

"Devin, stop…"

"What'chu mean stop! You don't love me anymore?" He asked, kissing me.

"Come on now Devin, I can't stop loving you," I said enjoying his kiss.

'What was wrong with me? Carmen, don't fall for it again. No, I should give him another chance, we have a family.' So many thoughts went through my mind.

"I know I messed up. I've done a lot of crazy stuff in the past, but I'm going to change. I'm going to make you Mrs. Diaz, real soon."

After his bull crap speech, he started kissing me all over. Despite the smack to my face I couldn't resist him making love to me. Hitting me and then making love to me became the norm. It was confusing and couldn't be explained, but I just let it be. At times I wondered how many other women experienced the same thing.

I loved having sex and was in love with everything about Devin, despite the bad. Besides, before I met him I had never been in a relationship for more than a couple of months. I thought sex was the only thing men had to offer, and I wasn't interested in a relationship seeing how my parents' marriage failed.

Unfortunately, I was introduced to sex at a very young age. I was only seven and didn't fully understand what was happening. I was told it was a secret, and what we were doing was special, because I was special.

What was in his pants had me brain washed. I thought when we made love he wouldn't be interested in anyone else. I hated him, loved him, was in love with him, and then hated him again. I didn't know how to break the cycle. Although I was saying no with my mouth, the way he touched me had me screaming, "Yes!!!"

It still took him a while before he accomplished his task to get me upstairs. I felt like such an idiot. But after a while I followed him upstairs where we made love until we fell asleep.

When I woke up at 1:15 a.m. Devin was nowhere to be found. "This is some mess; I am so tired of him making me look like his fool. Where is my cell phone?" When I called he picked up on the first ring. "Wus'up baby?"

I could hear the music and the wind as he drove. "Devin, where are you? Why didn't you wake me when you left?"

"Oh, you were asleep, so I ran to get something to eat, do you want something?

His moments were more like two to three hours. "No that's okay; I'm going down to the club for a few hours to work. I'll see you when I get home."

"Okay that's cool babe. Be careful, I'll be home soon. I love you. I know I messed up, but I meant what I said Mrs. Diaz."

As he spoke I started to smile. He gave me that warm fuzzy feeling when he called me Mrs. Diaz. "I'm going to make this right with us, and let's not forget about little Devin, when he comes in the future. We'll live happily ever after.,"

I wanted to be mad, but I couldn't. "I know babe, you're just stressed, think positive and something will come through soon. But Devin, you can't relapse when things aren't going your way. It will get better; you have to believe that. I love you too, good night."

"You always know the right words to say to your man to lift his spirits. You're right, it has to get better."

Overcoming The Battle

Chapter Three

You would have thought everyone in Houston was at the club tonight. I ain't even mad because that means a good cash flow. "Carmen, what's up baby girl, let me get something strong on the rocks." It was Mr. Gigolo. His real name was Chris, but we called him that because every weekend he came to the club with a different woman.

"Do you want coke with that Chris?"

"Nah, just straight up, it's my man's birthday and we are getting wasted tonight," he said high- fiving his buddy.

"Okay, well y'all take it easy," I said placing his drink on the bar.

"Thank you," he said grabbing his drink. I made it my business to be the best bartender because of customers like Chris who left me twenty and thirty dollar tips. Then there were the ones that came in who didn't know how to have a good time. They would get drunk and cause such a commotion people started looking for other places to go. We must have been the best place in town because the crowd seemed to grow bigger every week.

"Aye girl, let me get a drink!" It was none other than Cristal, the sloppy drunk who stayed in everybody's business.

"Cristal, you do not need anything else to drink, chill out," her friend Shannon said while trying to pull her away from the bar.

"Shannon, you're not the drink patrol, I'm grown," she snatched away.

"Hey, I'm Carmen, what can I get for you ladies?"

Though I didn't know Cristal personally, I had heard about her and seen her around at the club a few times. Shannon looked at me shaking her head. I knew Shannon through Devin's mother, and she didn't seem like the type that would hang out with someone like Cristal.

"Carmen, please don't give Cristal anything else to drink. She's already been drinking over at Justin T's tonight, she doesn't need anymore."

Cristal was known to be a trouble making, rumor spreading girl who everyone disliked. She was a big liar and her mother was such an alcoholic she named her after expensive champagne, but Cristal carried herself pretty cheap.

"Hey, I know you, you're Devin's girl, right?" Cristal asked pushing Shannon out of the way.

"Yes I am. Now, what can I get you?"

"Ha! Ha! Ha! Okay, okay...you're his main girl right?" She laughed a drunken laugh.

"I'm his only girl. Can I get you anything? There are other customers I need to serve," I said getting a little irritated.

"I'm thinking, I'll let you know," she said brushing me off. As I turned to serve someone else, she started again. "Aye, Main Girl, we just saw Devin down at Justin T's Bar all hugged up on your sister. Yeah, that's right, your sister."

"Girl, please," I said rolling my eyes.

"Yes, your sister...the one you're with all the time. I know she's your sister," she said in a drunken stupor.

"Cristal, hush girl, you've been drinking too much," Shannon said trying to get her friend to keep quiet.

"Don't shush me; you know I'm not lying. You know it's the truth, you saw him too."

"Look, Cristal, Gin & Juice, whatever your name is. My sister is at home with my kids, and my man is in our bed asleep for your information." I tried my best not to be rude, because I still wanted a tip if she ordered a drink.

"Well, I'll be dog-on; Devin Diaz got a twin at Justin T's kissing all on your sister like he 'bout to give her that business."

"Look, I know your type. The one that can't get a man, so your busy trying to break up happy homes, keeping yourself in everybody else's business. What'chu need to do is focus on yours."

"Look heifer, I'm just trying to be a friend and tell you about your man. I was trying to be nice and help you out since you're the blind one. But it's cool though, and you're right, he ain't my man, he supposed to be yours."

I walked away, because using my energy for her was not something I was up for. After serving about three more customers I needed to take a break. "Carmen, where are you going? There are too many people for you to be walking away from the bar." Henry Findley the owner said when he saw me head to the ladies' room. He always said I was his best bartender and that I kept the people buying drinks, so I needed to be behind the bar at all times.

"Henry I'm going to pee, is that okay?" I said, shaking my head.

I could hear him yelling over the noise. "That's fine. Just make it quick, Kelley and Suzanne can't handle this crowd by themselves."

When I got to the bathroom I pulled my cell phone out and gave Devin a call. "Devin, where are you?" I asked as soon as I heard his voice on the other line.

"I was sleep until you woke me up."

"Where all did you go tonight? That girl Cristal in here claiming you was hugged up on some girl at Justin T's tonight."

"Man, that girl lying, ain't nobody been to Justin T's. I told you, I went to go get something to eat, afterwards I came right back to the house. You better stop letting them females fill your head with lies. You know how people do, they like to start drama."

"I just wanted to ask, even though I figured she was lying. Alright, it'll probably be around 6:30, when I get home."

"Okay Mrs. Diaz, I love you and I'll be here waiting on you."

I really liked him calling me that. "Love you too," I smiled.

****

"Hello?"

"Justin, it's me."

"Me who?"

"Man, this Devin, I need you to look out for me?"

"Oh, yeah man, what'chu need?"

"Dude, if you happen to run into Carmen, I wasn't there tonight."

"Okay D, I got you man, no problem. Holla at me later."

"Okay, good looking out."

Let me rest up so I can prepare for round three when Mrs. Diaz gets home.

****

I wanted to believe Devin, but something in his voice didn't sound like he had been awakened from his sleep. Even though Cristal was known to tell lies, she seemed so confident when she spoke, which made me believe there may have been some truth to it. My grandmother used to always say, "When drunken people speak, you should listen, because it's probably true."

Right now, I just need to shake it off and try not to worry about it. It took me a minute to get myself together. Despite the fight, we had a good night and I wasn't going to let some chick that I cared nothing about ruin it.

When I returned to the bar Shannon and her trouble making friend were gone. "Hey gorgeous, let me get three bottles of those right there," a guy said pointing at the green bottles behind me.

"That'll be $330.00," I said wanting to make sure he knew the price.

The nice-looking gentlemen handed me five one hundred dollar bills. "Make sure you keep the change," he said with the most charming smile I had ever seen.

That was the biggest tip I had received all night. Actually, it was the biggest tip I had ever received. "Thanks, I appreciate it." I said putting the change in my money pouch. He could tell from the look on my face that his tip was very generous. That money was going back into the old purse in a different part of the closet.

"What's your name?"

"Carmen."

"My name is Chad; I'm pretty well known around the city.

Chad was sexy, with blonde hair and those chestnut brown eyes were so beautiful, but I wasn't giving him any play. The Rolex on his wrist, the way he was dressed, and the tip he had just left said he had money. And of course, I had heard of him, his parents owned a few farms in the area. "Chad, are your parents Cindy and Jerry Malone, the owners of The Malone Farms?"

"Yes, those are my folks. If no one knows me, you can best believe they know my parents. So, are you having a good night?"

"Well, Mr. Malone, my night is good, and my fiancée is waiting for me at home."

"Ms. Carmen, I was only trying to have a conversation, I'm not trying to push up on you. But since you mentioned a fiancée, um...where's your ring?"

"It's coming soon," I smiled and told him to have a good night. I then started cleaning up, hoping the crowd would die down soon so I could leave a little early. I turned back around and he was still there.

"Does this fiancée of yours make you happy?"

"Yes of course, why would you ask that?"

"No disrespect, but you look a little stressed. A beautiful woman like you shouldn't look so stressed out."

"Excuse me?"

'Wow, did I really look like I had a rough night?' I thought to myself. *'Stressed?'* I didn't realize my mask didn't cover up what I'd gone through earlier.

"I'm not trying to get all in your business, but you're beautiful and deserve only the best, don't settle for anyone less. I hope you enjoy the rest of your night, take care. By the way Miss Lady, make sure that man puts a ring on your finger soon before you keep giving him a title. No disrespect, it's all love."

At first, I was a little offended, but as Chad walked away I realized he was only being genuine. However, his words made me question if I was settling. I had heard about the girl he dated who had broken his heart. There were talks around town that he was a really good man and would be a great husband to the woman he ended up with.

While I cleaned the other side of the bar a familiar voice caught my attention. "Girrrrlllllllll, get me your best drink on the house of course." Savannah sat at the bar ready to be served, a few free drinks, and she looked to be in a better mood.

Her boyfriend Carlos had purchased her a fully loaded, candy apple red Lexus ES 350 for Valentine's Day, but lately had stopped making payments and the repo man came and got it. She didn't know it had a tracking device on it, and that's how they found it at her residence. When she came out to go to work the repo driver was still hooking her car to his tow truck.

Savannah kept trying to call Carlos to tell him what was going on, but he wouldn't answer her call. The driver told her there was nothing he could do. He had an order from the finance company to pick it up and once it was paid then she could come get it.

Carlos texted Savannah about an hour after her vehicle was repossessed and told her their fling was over. He said he was making things right in his marriage and decided that he was going to be faithful to his wife. Savannah was livid; she could care less if he wanted to make things right with his wife. She actually thought it was great that he was married, that way she wasn't pressured into a commitment.

I couldn't blame her for not wanting to get into a full-time relationship with him. The main reason being that he was a married man, but there were some other reasons as well. Carlos had stained yellow teeth, and the biggest beer belly I had ever seen. He wasn't attractive at all, but he had money and that's all that mattered to her. He showered her with gifts and all she had to do was give him occasional hugs and kisses. As long as she made him feel important the gifts kept coming.

Now she needed $2,100.00 to get her car back. It was a good thing she still had her Honda Accord. It may not have been what she wanted, but it was transportation. "What brings you out tonight?" I asked seeing the change in her mood.

"Girl, I had to get out of that house, so I went to Justin T's for about an hour, and then decided to come here for a little bit. I didn't know you were working tonight. Who was that guy that just left, from what I saw of him, he was a cutie? But you know I love my chocolate, otherwise I would see about him."

"Girl you are crazy!" I laughed. "Anyway, his name is Chad. And yes, I decided to come in for a few hours. Let me ask you a question?"

"You know you can ask me anything? What's up?"

"Did you see Devin down at Justin T's?" I asked, hoping to verify Cristal's accusations.

"I don't think so, I was looking for winners, not losers," she laughed.

"Girl please, no one's perfect, we all make mistakes. Besides, he's been calling me Mrs. Diaz, so you know what that means."

"Honey, after eight years, you should already be Mrs. Diaz."

"Savannah!"

"Sorry, I was thinking out loud."

"It's cool, apology accepted." But I figured she was lying.

"Okay, Okay, that's good then. I'm happy if you're happy," she said sounding sincere.

"Thanks Savannah, it means a lot to have your support."

"You know they say some dogs can change and become well trained," she laughed again.

"Savannah, stop it!"

"I'm teasing, but enough about you and Devin, I have something to tell you."

"Okay, the spotlight is on you."

"I met a guy earlier at the gas station before I went to Justin T's. His name is Theodore. He drives a black Mercedes Benz, C Class. He's about maybe thirty-five and moved here a year ago from Killeen, Texas. Girl, he is the finest thing I've seen in a long time. We talked for an hour at the gas station and he wants to take me to that five-star steakhouse restaurant off Fifth and Broad Street. So those are my lunch plans tomorrow."

I rested at the bar and leaned towards her while she spoke, and was glad the crowd was dying down. "Are you talking about Eskos Steakhouse?"

"Yep, that's the one."

"Girl, I heard it's nice. Have you been there before?"

"Nope, but I can't wait to see how it is," she said taking a sip of her Malibu and pineapple drink. I knew it was her favorite, so I didn't have to ask what she wanted.

"Alright now, I like him already," I said, giving her a high-five.

"Yes Carmen, I believe he may be a winner and guess what?"

"What?"

"I'm even going to hold out for maybe a month or so before I let him get into my candy box," she laughed.

"You are just too crazy. I don't know what I'm going to do with you."

"Carmen, you know there is nothing you or anyone else can do to keep me tamed. Let me get out of here, I have to go to work in the morning."

"Be safe Savannah, and drive carefully."

"I will friend, good night, you do the same," she said walking out of the club.

Savannah knew how to play men to get what she wanted, but she mainly involved herself with men who were already taken. She said it was fun and she didn't have to worry about a man trying to keep tabs, so she could do whatever, whenever.

I can't say I agreed, but she was my best friend, so I didn't judge her. She was always there for me when I needed a shoulder to cry on. She carried herself with so much confidence, and could get whatever she wanted from any man.

It was like a game she played. She felt as though a man couldn't really love her, so she gave them sex and they would buy her things in exchange. Savannah was a gorgeous twenty-five-year-old who looked like a Puerto Rican goddess. She had a beautiful toned complexion, shoulder length curly hair, and the smallest waist and curviest hips that made all the guys fall in love with her at first sight.

Growing up she had experienced some traumatic moments in her life, but she didn't share much. She had seen her mother with multiple men. Her mother had been married four times and divorced them all by the time Savannah was sixteen.

Savannah saw her mother get what she wanted out of men. I guess you could say her mother taught her well. The day she left her last husband she blamed Savannah for it. I wasn't sure of the whole story, but she did say her mom told her not to tell anyone.

I guess she was ashamed since it was her fourth marriage ending. Savannah and her mother hadn't really connected and hadn't had a relationship since that day. She had even asked her mother if they could go to counseling, but she refused.

Since Savannah was the oldest of seven children, her mother partied all the time and would leave her to babysit her siblings – she was never home. As soon as one of the guys in the neighborhood saw her mother leave they would come knocking at the back door. She would have sex with the older guys in the neighborhood as long as they gave her money in exchange. She didn't have much, so she put her skills to work in order to get clothes and shoes. Since Savannah watched some of the children in her neighborhood, her mom assumed that's where the money came from.

I wondered how someone could keep going after all of that. One thing for sure, Savannah was a strong woman and could not be broken.

Overcoming The Battle

Chapter Four

Henry asked me to stay a little later, so I didn't get home until about 7:30 a.m. I slid on the outfit I had purchased the day before. As we cuddled in bed, Devin whispered in my ear, "Carmen, I love you so much. I've been thinking all night, and I can't think of anything else than making you my wife."

"I love you too Devin, I can't imagine my life without you."

I felt him getting excited while he was holding me. What was it about this man that had me so in love with him? I felt I needed him and would be incomplete without him. Was it the children, or was it because I hadn't been in a relationship with anyone as long as he and I had been together?

If that's the case, would that make him my comfortable mate instead of my soul mate? I was so comfortable with him that I was afraid to leave. Thinking of my soul loving someone else seemed impossible. We had an eight-year history and I couldn't imagine being with anyone else. Of course, we had our issues, but they always seemed to work themselves out. I wanted my children to be raised in a two-parent household. I wanted the girls to receive the love from their father that I never received from mine, so I was willing to stay.

Growing up, one of the worst feelings was hoping my dad would be my hero. Instead he was like the thief in the night that came and took my heart out of my chest, broke it into pieces, and buried it. I'm grown now, and I've put the past behind me, but I didn't want that for my daughters.

Devin spoke softly, preparing to make love to me, but Cristal's conversation replayed in my mind. I dismissed the allegations concerning my man, refusing to allow other women or anyone else for that matter end our relationship. Ignoring her voice, I focused on the task at hand. Devin was making love to me, and that's all that mattered at the moment.

The next day we picked Mackenzie and Taylor up from Charlotte's house and went to visit his mother. She and I didn't have the best relationship. Whenever she was in my presence it was hard for me to hold my tongue. It took everything in me not to be disrespectful.

Although we didn't get along I had to admit, the woman had skills with a comb and brush. She could style some hair: from Hispanic, African-American, Caucasian, you name it, and I guarantee Adriana Diaz could do it. She owned two beauty salons, and was known to be one of the best hair stylists in Texas.

Adriana was very protective over her son and would do anything for him. I admired the way she kept her family close. Devin's father passed when his mother was pregnant with him, so I guess that made her such a pit bull.

Adriana never knew any of his father's family members, but he wanted to know more about his African American heritage. Devin had a lot of black friends, thinking it would help him better understand the culture.

Unfortunately, most of his friends lived in subsidized housing which involved drugs and a high crime rate.

Devin, on the other hand grew up in the suburbs, but quickly got involved with the wrong crowd and started selling drugs. Being a drug dealer was not a good career for him. Once he tried his own product he started using more than he sold.

Despite her son's pitfalls the love she expressed for him was something I wished we had in our family. Watching her interact with Devin and the girls made me think of my grandmother Mrs. Stella, my mother's mom. For years I tried reaching out to her by writing letters, but got no response. She wasn't interested in a relationship with her biracial grandchildren. Just like Pretty Boy, I wished I had that grandmother-granddaughter relationship. Maybe if I did my life would have turned out differently.

When we got to his mother's she had been waiting at the door for us – well, him and the twins. "Mijo!" She kissed him all over his face.

I noticed the look on her face when she saw me standing behind him. Her expression always said, "Why are you here?" Trust me it wasn't because I wanted to be, but since he was my man, it was my duty to be by his side.

After giving me the stink eye, her face lit up when she turned her attention to Mackenzie and Taylor. "Hija! Hija! I missed my adorable grandbabies," she said in her Hispanic accent. "Hi Carmen," she said in English.

"Hello Mrs. Diaz, how are you?" I asked, but really didn't care.

"I'm fine, thank you," she grunted.

I really hated going to her house, she was so disrespectful. I tried to get along with her for the sake of Devin, but she was relentless. "I love the flowers you planted out front," I said trying to break the ice.

"Thanks," she said, not looking my way.

"Devin, how long are we going to be here? I don't know if I can deal with your mother's antics today."

"What did you say, Carmen?"

"You heard me Adriana! I'm sick of you disrespecting me!"

"Well, I would respect you, but you have no class! I don't understand what my son sees in you. What kind of mother talks about their kids' grandmother in front of her children?"

"No class…really, you never think about the children when you're acting like a disrespectful witch!"

"Mama!!! Carmen!!!! I'm not having this today! Y'all acting like some kids!" he said shaking his head, walking towards the back yard.

Adriana grabbed the girls and followed. "Come on babies; let's go with daddy to the back yard so Mimi can show you what I got for you."

Adriana blamed me for everything. She claimed when Devin moved to Florida to attend college he came back a different person when he got involved with me. From my understanding he was that way before he ever went to Florida.

Devin's Aunt Isabel came from the kitchen wearing an apron and cooking gloves. "Hello beautiful," She greeted with hugs and kisses.

"Aunt Isabel, the food smells amazing."

Aunt Isabel was Adriana's twin sister. She was always a breath of fresh air. Aunt Isabel was absolutely gorgeous, with hair that flowed down to the middle of her back. She was a wise Christian woman who had such a loving spirit. You would have thought she was an angel sent from heaven living here on earth. She was always inviting me to church, but I kept telling her I wasn't ready. She was positive that one day I would tell her "yes."

"Carmen, every time I see you, you look even more stunning. How is that nephew of mine treating you?"

"Things are great Aunt Isabel," I said dropping my head.

"Are things really great, or is that the picture you're painting in your head?"

"Yes, Aunt Isabel, they really are!"

"So, everything is fine?" She questioned looking over the top of her glasses.

"Yes, Aunt Isabel, I promise. Everything is fine."

"Everything, Carmen?"

"Yes, yes, Aunt Isabel, everything."

"I think you're a bright beautiful lady, you don't deserve a man treating you like you're his opponent in a boxing match."

Aunt Isabel knew I was lying. A few months ago, she came by the house to see the girls and for some reason the door was slightly open. When she walked in she saw her nephew knocking me around like a punching bag. Ever since that day she never let me forget it.

When she told Adriana about the incident, Adriana assured Aunt Isabel it must have been something I did to cause him to react in such a way.

Although I may not have taken heed, I loved to sit and listen to her wisdom. "Senorita, let me ask you a serious question?

"Okay, sure?"

"Do you know how a man is supposed to treat you?"

I couldn't get my mouth to work. She must have thought I was taking too long, so she went right to her next question. "Do you love you, more than you love that man?"

I thought it was an interesting question, but again I did not know how to respond. "See Senorita, sometimes as women, we tend to put all of our love into a man and forget what it means to love ourselves first."

"Carmen, when you love yourself, and know who you are, you'll know what you're supposed to receive from a man. More importantly, you'll know what you are not supposed to receive. You have to know your worth, if not than others will define it for you and that's what you'll settle for."

Everything Aunt Isabel said was absolutely true, and I totally understood why she was concerned. She was still thinking about the old Devin. "Aunt Isabel, Devin has changed. And yes, I love myself, but I also love him. Maybe, I love us the same, I don't know. He's even talking about marriage. I promise he really has changed. He wants to make this work for our family."

I thought my speech was convincing, her eyes looked a little sad. "Well, Senorita that's great. I really hope he has changed and everything works out," she smiled.

"Aunt Isabel, we are so happy right now. Things couldn't be better," I said now trying to convince myself.

"Okay, come with me while I finish the Pastelon de Platano Maduro," she said walking towards the kitchen.

"Now Aunt Isabel, you know I do not know what that is," I laughed.

"It's a sweet plantain casserole. You're going to love it. The ingredients are ground beef, yellow plantains, peppers, cheese, and lots of other yummy stuff. You must stay for dinner."

Devin peaked into the kitchen when he saw us talking. "Carmen, I have to get something from the store. I'll be right back. Aunt Isabel, it smells good," he said when he saw her cut her eye at him.

'What could he have needed from the store?' I thought? We went to the store before we came to his mother's house. Thoughts of him being up to no good ran through my mind, but I quickly dismissed them.

"Don't be gone too long sobrino, we are ready to eat," Aunt Isabel instructed. She must have known what I was thinking.

"I'll be right back, it's important, love y'all."

Surprisingly, he returned just like he said. During dinner Adriana was so engaged in her conversation with

Devin, the twins, and her sister, you would have thought I wasn't even in the room. "Mijo, guess what?"

"What's that Ma?"

"One of my client's husband is the Vice President at the Steinhouser Manufacturing Company. They make parts for luxury vehicles. She said all you have to do is apply and the job is yours. Here's his card and the website where you can apply. Call him after you put in your application. It's in the Northern part of Texas, but I'm sure you won't mind the drive since the starting pay is $60,000.00."

"$60,000!!! Are you serious?"

"Yes," Adriana smiled shaking her head.

"Thanks, so much Mama; I'm going to apply as soon as we get home!"

"Baby, you said it, this right here is the beginning of better," he said holding up the card, kissing me on my cheek. "Thank you for always encouraging me and sticking by my side," he kissed me again.

"Mijo, finish your dinner. You two can save that stuff for when you get home. We are having family time right now," she said sarcastically.

'This woman is such a hater,' I thought.

"I'm glad you said that and you're right, it is family time. Mama, things are going to change with how you treat Carmen. I love her, and this is who I'm going to be with."

Devin stood from the table, pushed his chair back and walked out to the car. The look on her face was priceless. It was going to take an army to help her pick her face up off the floor. She couldn't believe he was defending me – I couldn't believe it. "That's right Adriana; you heard what my man said." I couldn't help myself as she sat with the dumbest look on her face.

Devin came back with two dozen roses, walked over to me and got down on one knee. "Devin, what are you doing?" I smiled. At that moment I could barely contain myself.

"Carmen Wilson, we have been through thick and thin. I love you so much and I'm so sorry for the past, but my life would not be complete unless you say "yes" to be my wife. Carmen, will you marry me?"

"Yes! Yes! Yes, I will marry you!" I grabbed his neck and almost choked him, I was so happy. Finally, my dream was coming true.

The ring was the most beautiful ring I had seen. I wondered if someone helped him pick it out. Come to find out he hadn't stolen the money at all for drugs, he had been saving for the ring before he lost his job, so he borrowed the money from the stash in the closet to purchase my engagement ring.

He had purchased it a week ago. But I guess he felt bad about how he screwed up and decided to do it now. He told me not to worry; he was going to put the money back once he started back working. Devin was determined to prove to me that he was a changed man.

There was no way I could doubt him now. *'So that's why he started calling me Mrs. Diaz.'* I had forgiven him for the mistakes he had made the day before. Now I was ready to move forward and start planning our wedding. If I could just keep him away from those stupid friends of his, we would be alright.

I could see Adriana out of the corner of my eye; she couldn't believe her son was serious. "Mijo, I had no idea, I thought you would have mentioned it to me first. But, if this is what you want, then congratulations."

"Yes, it's what he wants Adriana, or he wouldn't have asked. It's time for you to start learning how to respect me. Whether you like it or not, I am going to be your daughter-in-law."

The nerve of her to think he should have spoken with her first. But, not even Adriana was about to ruin my moment. "Mama and Carmen, you both are going to start showing some respect for one another."

"Mama, to be honest, it's you most of the time. I don't know what it is you have against Carmen, but I love her. She and the twins are my world, and this is who I'm going to be with. Do you understand?"

"Si, Mijo. You are right. I apologize for my behavior, I'm going to do better," she said as she walked over to kiss him.

"Daddy and Mommy are getting married," Aunt Isabel said to the girls.

"Are they really?" Mackenzie asked with the biggest smile.

"Yes, they are, and you two are going to be the prettiest flower girls ever."

"Congratulations, Carmen and Devin," Aunt Isabel said with a hug. "I pray for blessings and a beautiful marriage for you guys. Remember the key is to keep God first."

"I bought a cake Aunt Isabel, will you help with it?"

"Of course, Devin," she said walking into the kitchen with him.

When they left the room, I turned to Adriana to have an adult conversation with her. "Look Adriana, you heard what Devin said. It's time to cut this mess out; I'm willing to try if you are."

Adriana looked away as I spoke. Regardless of how she felt about me, she really wanted to be happy for her son. "I am willing to try for my son," she agreed. We shook hands, but I could tell it was going to be a process.

Overcoming The Battle

Chapter Five

It had been three months since Devin proposed, and he couldn't wait for me to be his wife. He would tease me and say we should book a flight to Las Vegas and get married, but he knew that wasn't the type of wedding I wanted. We had already decided our colors would be pink, blue, and white. I could already see my bridesmaids in their dresses, and the ice sculptures would be carved into our initials C & D. I couldn't wait for the day to come when I became Mrs. Devin Diaz. Things were going good and I prayed daily it stayed that way.

Devin was hired at Steinhouser Manufacturing Company with a starting salary of $70,000. After he got the job he said I no longer had to work so hard. He said it made him feel like less of a man with his lady working two jobs.

Quitting Dynamics Wireless was the best thing I could have ever done. It felt like a ton of bricks had been lifted from my shoulders. For the first time I could experience being a stay-at-home mom. Although, planning the wedding, felt like a full-time job, my daily schedule consisted of cooking, cleaning, watching cartoons, and learning DVDs with the girls.

Aunt Isabel never gave up on me. She continued to invite me to church until I finally gave in. On the first Sunday we attended, Pastor Brian C. Richardson's message made me feel like I could do anything with my life, *"If you believed nothing was impossible, you would see the impossible happen."* The twins were excited and looked forward to

Sunday mornings. Mackenzie and Taylor enjoyed the Children's church where they were learning a lot about God and His love.

We had been attending every Sunday for the last two and a half months, but if only Devin would come with us, we could be a complete family. Every Sunday he gave a different excuse as to why he couldn't go, but promised he would try the following week.

Thanks to the pastor and his messages, I decided to give my life to Christ. Even though I said "yes," I didn't fully understand what I was doing, but believed this was a change that I needed. "It's a process Carmen, just take it one day at a time, seek God daily and He will show you His will and the way for your life," Aunt Isabel said with tears of joy. Then she instructed me to read my Bible, pray, and start listening to Godly music.

I must admit, it took me a minute to understand Praise and Worship, but the encounter of the presence of God was amazing. In fact, it was so amazing it can't be explained only experienced. But, one of the hardest things was abstaining from sex, over eating, and everything else I never wanted to say "no" to. Thinking about Aunt Isabel words, "God will show you His will and the way for your life," I started praying and seeking God to show me and to replace my desires and will with His desires and will.

Since starting a relationship with God, my view about sex had changed. I expected my conversation with Devin to go a little different when I decided to talk to him about it. "Devin, we need to talk"

"You wanna talk; because we can be upstairs in the bed *talking* in a minute," he said smiling

"That's actually what I want to talk about – us having sex."

"What's going on with us having sex?"

"Devin, I've decided since I'm working on my relationship with God, I want to do the right thing and wait until we marry before we have sex again."

"Carmen, you sound silly, we're engaged, and we already have children. I'm sure God won't mind," he said kissing me on the cheek.

I leaned back with a serious look on my face. "Wait a minute, you for real?"

"Yes, I am. I'm going to be celibate and I've already made a commitment to God."

"Man, you done started going to church and now you just want to cut me off. What about my needs?"

"Devin, we are getting married in a few months, isn't our love stronger than sex."

"Alright man, whatever. I'm going down to the lounge to hang out with the boys, I'll be back later."

"Devin, can I trust you to be faithful until then? It's only sex."

"How about you pray about it," he said as he walked out of the house slamming the door behind him.

Our conversation had me second guessing my decision. Maybe it would be okay since we are about to get married. But I had been reading the Bible, and when it started talking about fornication I saw sex in a different manner.

Now I wanted to commit my body to God until marriage, understanding sex was a beautiful creation for marriage.

Pastor Brian spoke on *"Marriage,"* one Sunday and explained how God intended sex for marriage. He explained how the world took what God intended for us to enjoy and abused it. He also said when a man and a woman have sex they become one. He said it was one of several ways a soul tie was formed, and the two souls are knitted together. Soul ties have a major effect on your spiritual life. A soul tie could cause people to continue to carry a person's soul with them even after their dealings with them are finished.

After listening to his message, I saw sex in a totally different light. I know now that it's not just about pleasure and feelings, but the emotions that come with two spirits becoming one. I no longer wanted to be one with Devin as his girlfriend, but I wanted that oneness that came with being his wife. And of course, Devin didn't agree.

After our conversation he still tried. While we slept he held me, started rubbing my thighs, and then tried to remove my clothing. He knew I was serious when I started sleeping in my robe. Some nights it would be burning up, but even if I had to sweat off a couple of pounds, it was worth it.

I was determined we were not going to have sex; breaking my vow with God is not an option. Though I had to admit, it wasn't the easiest thing to do. But I took it one day at a time, just like Aunt Isabel said. Every day I looked forward to the next.

Every day I read my Bible, put on praise and worship music and worshipped God. I made it a point to have my devotion and subsequently was encouraged by quality over quantity. I'm thankful that Aunt Isabel never stop opening up to me about God. She was very excited about my new walk. She prayed with me that Devin and I would put God first in our marriage.

In order for us to put God first, Devin and I would have to at least start praying together, but he wasn't really interested. Since he had been working, his job was his god. He never had a job making the kind of money he was making. Now, he could pay the bills, and have money left over to put in our savings account. I felt confident Devin would change and start going to church with us real soon. I refused to give up on him.

Overcoming The Battle

Chapter Six

I hadn't seen much of Savannah since she started dating her new man. Her face lit up when she spoke of him, when we would video chat. Since she started dating Theodore she even stopped communicating with all the other men in her life, she said he satisfied all her needs.

Savannah's mother told her she was worthless and would never have a man of her own. Now, she was a one-man-woman, this was definitely a new Savannah. All she talked about was her king. "Theodore this and Theodore that." All I could picture was the two of them wearing crowns.

Today, Savannah, Theodore and I were meeting for lunch. I was so anxious to see my best friend. While finishing my chores I smiled thinking about the joy Savannah had in her voice when she called the day before. She said everyone was happy for her except her mother of course. She told Savannah she better watch out for men, they were not to be trusted. A few months ago, her mother had been diagnosed with HIV. After receiving the news, she became very bitter.

I was ready to meet Mr. Theodore, especially since he was the one paying. Walking inside of Amazing Shrimp & Fish Seafood Restaurant, I noticed they had done some remodeling. As soon as I walked through the door I could see Savannah interacting with her new man. I could tell she was really in love with him, she was so engaged, staring at him face to face. "Hey, my friend," she said while standing up to give me a hug.

There was a glow about her that sparkled like a diamond, she was so happy. I also couldn't help but notice she had gained a little weight. Not much, but I could tell in her hips and butt, which I couldn't have imagined getting any bigger.

"Hello," the gentleman stood to shake my hand. "I'm Theodore. You must be Carmen; I've heard a lot about you. It's good to finally meet you." Theodore was handsome; tall, very clean cut, spoke with a confident tone, and his tailor-made suit looked like it cost more than everything in my closet. And a beautiful smile, when he smiled it lit up the room.

We sat for about an hour while I enjoyed the sweet buttery biscuits. At first Savannah laughed when I asked 8 out of 10 questions I had lined up. She wasn't surprised because I did that to most of the men she dated. "Carmen, oh my gosh; I cannot believe you, stop it."

Even though I asked as many questions as I could, there wasn't anything I could find out of place with him. While we talked, he looked at me like I was supposed to stop eating my biscuits. But trust me I didn't. "Savannah, I was just wrapping up my interview," I laughed.

Amazing Shrimp & Fish used to be me and Devin's favorite restaurant, but after he lost his job we couldn't afford it. We hadn't gotten around to going since things were back on track. I couldn't wait to get back home to tell him about the wonderful time I had so he could bring me back. I know he and Savannah didn't get along, so I'd have to skip some of the details. But I had to make sure he knew how much I missed our favorite dining spot.

Theodore had crossed all his "T's" and dotted all his "I's" as far as I was concerned. He spoke with such integrity about goals and a vision for his life. I was very intrigued. He made me wish Devin could carry on a conversation like that. "So, what are your dreams and goals Carmen?" He asked as though he was curious to know.

I battled with trying to figure out who I was all my life, so my dreams and goals was something I had no clue of. I knew I always wanted more in life, but never talked about a vision or goals. "To be honest, I'm really not sure at the moment."

"Well, one thing I'm certain of, we shouldn't settle for anything. If you feel like there is more to life, it's because there is." he assured me.

Having that type of conversation with Devin was pointless. He wasn't interested in my goals, let alone my dreams. Every time I tried to talk to him he would either ignore me or change the subject. He believed our lives played out according to the cards we were dealt, and there was nothing we could do to change it.

Theodore said he didn't have the best life, but now he's making almost seven figures. He made me believe a bad deck of cards could be played out fairly. Maybe, it was possible for things to change and we didn't have to accept the cards life dealt us. "It's not about where you came from in life, let it be your motivation. It's about where you are going in life, and that should be your focus," Theodore continued.

I couldn't wait to tell Devin about Theodore. I really wanted them to meet. Theodore could teach Devin a thing or two. Even though Savannah and Devin didn't get along, we still went out on double dates from time to time. Devin made sure to let me know he was only doing it for me.

After listening to Theodore, it gave me hope. He had my approval to continue seeing my friend. Who was I kidding? Savannah wouldn't have stopped dating him even if I were totally against it. Besides, I couldn't let my trust issues interfere with her happiness.

After we ate Theodore said he had to go by the office to complete some performance reviews. Once again, I was impressed. "Carmen, I'm so glad you joined us."

"So am I. It was a pleasure meeting you." After he left I couldn't wait to talk to Savannah. We stood by her car as we watched him drive off. I almost couldn't contain my excitement. "Savannah, it's good to see you so happy, you deserve it, I'm happy for you."

"Awe, come here and let me squeeze you. Thanks for being my friend. You have always accepted me, flaws and all. You love me like family."

"Just know I'm always here. Good night, I have to go pick up your god-daughters."

"Okay, good night and give my girls love for me." I closed the door smiling because we were both happily in love and nothing was going to change that.

A few nights later while playing board games with the girls the phone rang. "Carmen! Carmen!" Savannah screamed.

"Yes, calm down, what's going on?"

"I may be pregnant; I think I'm going to be a mommy!"

"Wow, Savannah! That's great news; oh my gosh! Congratulations!"

"I know right, but I won't know for sure until my appointment tomorrow."

As I listened to her, I couldn't help but rejoice. Thank goodness if she were pregnant it wouldn't be by somebody's husband or boyfriend. Theodore was unlike any man Savannah had been with. Now, she was having a baby by the man of her dreams. What more could she ask for?

Savannah also told me her cousin Tammy had called her two weeks ago and said she was expecting. When Savannah asked who the father was, Tammy started laughing. Evidently, that was her way of saying she didn't know.

It was just like Tammy to sleep around with several men at a time. I never cared for Tammy; she was always throwing herself on Devin, even in front of me. She was known to be the town's slut. I swear that girl was going to make me catch a charge.

The next day, Savannah called me after her doctor's appointment. "Carmen, I'm having a baby! The doctor said I'm nine weeks. I'm so excited! But, I'm also a little scared."

"Don't be scared. This is going to be an exciting adventure for you."

"Yeah, you're right."

"I'm so excited for you and Theodore. You guys are going to be great parents."

"I know he is excited too. I can't wait until we start shopping for the baby. Oh, I need a new wardrobe. I may be pregnant, but I will be pretty and pregnant. I will not be looking ratchet."

I laughed at Savannah, but I knew she was very serious." Welcome to motherhood friend, but unfortunately you're going to be shopping more for a little person than yourself now."

"Who me? We will be getting equal shopping sprees," she laughed.

"Well, congratulations again friend, but let me go ahead and get the girls settled. I will talk to you later."

"Okay Carmen, I'm in such a great mood, please tell Devin I said Hello."

That took me by complete surprise. "I sure will Savannah. Wait? Hello? Is this Savannah? The baby has changed you that quickly. It's a miracle!"

"You are silly Carmen. Goodnight love."

Chapter Seven

Every morning I awaken to the feeling of butterflies in my stomach. I couldn't believe in three months I was going to be Mrs. Devin Diaz. The girls and I had been in the mall for hours looking for a formal gown for Adriana's party. She was celebrating the opening of her third salon in Houston.

Our relationship had gotten a little better. Adriana and I were really trying for Devin's sake. We had even started going to breakfast several times where we talked about the wedding plans. I have to admit, she came up with some good ideas.

I really wanted to look nice for Adriana's event and wasn't sure if I should wear a short or long dress, open toed shoes or stilettos. I needed to decide quickly since the party was in two hours, and I still had to drop the girls off at Charlotte's. *Okay, I'm going to go with this purple short halter dress with the black sequence,'* I thought to myself. It was the perfect match with my black open toe heels. I really liked the peach dress, but unfortunately, they didn't have it in my size.

Everything I wanted didn't fit. My weight was something I never considered when my eating binges occurred. Most of my binges occurred due to my relationship with my father. Then there was the constant conflict with Devin.

As I went to put the peach dress back on its rack the sound of an annoying familiar voice approached me. "Oooh wee girl, look at those gorgeous little girls. I must say, you and Devin did a great job with these babies," she said starring Taylor and Mackenzie up and down.

With her hand on her hip she chewed her gum so hard you would have thought she hadn't eaten in days. As she chewed her gum it popped with a noise my ears couldn't stand to hear. "They look just like Devin. Girl, I'm telling you, the only part you played was carrying them," she laughed.

"Hi, my name is Cristal, how are you little ladies?" As the girls said hello, I had to keep my cool. It took everything in me not to curse her out. Then I had to remind myself that night at the club was old news.

God was turning my heart around, so I needed to be nice. It was apparent a change was taking place within me. Yes, the girls did look more like Devin and Adriana. They had Devin's shape, his complexion, and his chubby cheeks. They had Adriana's big bright smile, her eyes and curly dark hair that hung down their backs.

"Hello Cristal, we have to go."

"Hey, Devin's Girl, I had to find a dress for the party tonight. You know supporting my beautician is a must. Adriana has been keeping my hair looking good since middle school," she said referring to her fresh cut. "Girls, your grandmother can do some hair."

Cristal gave me a sad look when she saw the peach dress in my hand. "Girl, that dress is beautiful. It's the same one I purchased to wear tonight. Unfortunately, it doesn't come in XXX Large. They only go up to large; you may want to try the plus size boutique. I'm sure they have what you're looking for."

"Well, Cristal, that's not the size I wear. Besides, I like the other dress better, if you must know."

'How did she do that? She nailed my size right on the head.'

"Cristal, you don't even look like you eat. I would think you would be shopping in the little girl's section for something to wear."

"Ha! Devin's Girl, you are hilarious," she said rolling her eyes, and then went back to talking to the twins. "Your hair looks nice girls; Grandma must have done it. You would think your mother would take advantage of her skills."

'Okay, I'm just going to ignore her, she is trying to push my buttons and take me out of my happy place. I'm not going to let her do it.'

I laughed trying to forget about the comment she had just made. "We would love to chat, but we do have to hurry. Of course, I have to get ready to attend my mother-in-law's party," I said running my fingers threw my hair, making sure she noticed my engagement ring.

"Mother-in-law, let me see, is that a ring. Did Devin propose?!" She grabbed my hand and looked at my ring with a confused look. I could tell she thought it was nice and seemed a little jealous from the way her mouth twisted, and her nostrils flared. "Well that's nice, congratulations. I guess you got over him being all hugged up with your sister at Justin T's, huh?"

No, she didn't have the audacity to continue to disrespect me in front of my children. She must be crazy. Cristal was trying to get me to release the girl from Smithstone James, and I can guarantee she didn't want to meet her. The old Carmen would react first, then think later, but I'm better than that now.

There was a time when I used to have such a bad attitude, ready to fight when somebody said the wrong thing. I was very blunt and hurtful with my words, not caring who they affected. "Look Cristal, I feel sorry for women like you. Hopefully, one day you'll find a man, so you can experience the happiness I am experiencing. And going forward, if you see me, please don't speak. Act like I don't exist. Damn-it! I'm so tired of your jealousy and foolishness!"

Forgetting the twins were standing with me, her comment made me get out of character and a word slipped. I immediately heard Taylor say to Mackenzie, "Did mommy say a bad word?" Her eyes stretched widely as she shook her head,

"Yes, I think mommy did say a bad word," Mackenzie echoed.

They were completely shocked because they had never heard me speak like that before. I proceeded towards the checkout counter when I heard her say," Girl please, I could have had Devin twenty times if I wanted him."

Before I knew it, my middle finger was in the air. "Go to hell," I carefully formed my lips, so the girls didn't see what I was saying. Cristal had taken me to a place I was trying not to go. I ignored her laugh, paid for my items and hurried out of the store. Devin and I didn't need to be late for his mother's party.

When we got there Adriana had so many clients at her party and the crowds continued to arrive every five minutes. With the weather being so nice, the party was both inside and outside. She had even hired a catering company to host the event.

I had to admit, even though she hadn't won the best mother-in-law award, she was in the running for Best Event Planner of the Year. Adriana had completely out done herself. It was one of the best put together events I had ever attended. As I looked around her home, I was amazed at the decorations, flowers, and candles. The colors even matched the hostess' attire. Now I was ecstatic that she was helping with the wedding.

Devin's behavior quickly distracted my thoughts when I saw how much he was drinking. "Devin, I know this is your mother's party, but please don't keep drinking like that. I would hate for you to get drunk and embarrass her, not to mention me."

"Babe, I'm good, stop worrying. I've only had a little to drink, let's have a good time."

We walked towards the patio where I noticed Cristal standing by the foyer. Of course, she was wearing the long peach dress. Although I really wanted the dress, it was a good thing they didn't have my size. We would have been twins and that would have ruined my evening.

She rolled her eyes when I walked by, but knew not to say anything. Devin saw the look on my face and kissed me on the cheek. "I told you don't worry about these jealous females; they just want what you have."

When he kissed me, Cristal frowned and turned her head. After I told Devin about the incident at the mall, he told me how she had been making passes at him since high school. He said he'd even tried hooking her up with one of his friends, but it didn't work.

I knew she wanted my man, that's why she acted the way she did. Devin was right, I wasn't about to let her put a bad taste in my mouth. Cristal was not going to be my focus tonight.

As we walked towards Adriana he saw a guy and pointed at him. "Hey, I see that dude at my job. He's always walking through while everyone else works. It's like he owns the place or something."

The gentleman was with a beautiful woman, and I could tell they were a couple as he stood behind her with his hands around her waist while they spoke with Adriana. A few seconds later we were face to face. "Hey Mama, you look so, Bonita," Devin said kissing her on the cheek. He had just seen her earlier, but he acted like he hadn't seen her all week. I was a little worried that the alcohol was causing him to act a little strange.

"Mijo, Carmen, I would like for you to meet my client, Karen Hackford and her husband."

"Devin, Karen's husband is the guy I was telling you about. He's the Vice President at Steinhouser. He was the one who pulled the strings for you to get you hired so quickly, so you might want to thank him," she said smiling as she took a sip of her wine.

Adriana's client's husband looked like he had seen a ghost. Devin was quick to shake his hand. "Ah man, I was just telling my fiancée how I see you around at the plant. Thanks man for the job, I really appreciate it."

"No problem, it was a pleasure to be able to help," he returned the shake.

As he shook my hand I could feel the sweat on his palms. "Hello, my name is Theodore Hackford. It's nice to meet you." Theodore put on a good act with his introduction. Nobody would have known he and I had lunch together with his pregnant girlfriend. How could I tell my best friend that the man she was in love with and pregnant by, was married?

Overcoming The Battle

Chapter Eight

Devin and I hadn't been getting along for the past few weeks. If we weren't arguing about sex, it was about me telling Savannah about Theodore. After Adriana's party I felt really bad. I didn't want to be the dream crusher, but she had to know what she was about to embark upon.

When Devin and I got home after the party he started kissing me, and we ended up making love. I felt guilty, because I had broken my commitment to God. But the night was so elegant making love to him seemed to make it the perfect ending. Besides I thought it would take my mind off my friend, but the entire time I could only think about my friend.

I tried to get Devin to understand why I had to tell Savannah about Theodore. "Devin, if the shoe was on the other foot and it was your friend you would want them to know."

"If you want these bills to be paid you won't say anything to her,"

"God will make a way for these bills; besides he can't fire you because he is a lying cheating scum-bag."

"Carmen, that's not your business! I need this job, so don't say anything. Let her find out on her own."

"Devin, it's not right and you know it!"

"I'm done talking about it. That man got me a good job, and I'm going to keep it."

"Alright then, but I know one thing we will not be having sex again until we're married, and this time I'm serious."

"Carmen, I'm your man and your job is to take care of your man," he said sarcastically.

"Excuse me?"

"Trust me; having sex is not something I'm worried about?"

"What did you say?"

"I'm not explaining myself. I've said all I have to say."

"What does that mean Devin, are you cheating?"

"Baby look, I don't want to argue, and no I'm not cheating. I thought you were done accusing me of that?"

"Well, the look on your face was questionable!"

"Carmen, you know I love you. We will be married soon, so don't let other people's affairs come in between us. We don't need her drama in our house. Do you understand where I'm coming from?"

I understood why Devin didn't want me to say anything, but he didn't understand where I was coming from. This time it wasn't the fact that they didn't get along, Devin was afraid of losing money. I think the devil was trying to tempt me. The next day the phone rang, guess who? "Good morning Savannah."

"Girl, I couldn't wait to talk to you."

"I see. Do you know what time it is?" I yawned.

"I know it's early, but I was up, so I decided to call. How was the party last night?"

"Umm, it was good, just a party. Why you ask?"

"No reason, just asking. Sitting here with this smile tattooed to my face, I'm so excited Carmen! I can't wait to see who the baby is going to look like. Both parents are fine so the baby will be beautiful," she laughed. "Gosh, I love that man so much. It's like my whole life has changed since we met. He is the best boyfriend ever, and I'm sure he's going to be a great husband and father."

'Humph…going to be a great husband? He's already a husband,' I thought. I felt bad because I knew in a matter of minutes her entire world was about to fall apart.

"So, Theodore, my wonderful man and I just left the doctor's and found out we're having a girl!"

"Awe, how sweet Savannah, a baby girl."

"Carmen, I'm in love with her already. I can't wait to show her what a real mother's love is. I'm going to set a good example for her. She will never experience the things I did in life. I'm excited that she'll know her father and we will be a happy family."

At one point during our conversation I got so frustrated. "How are you going to do that?" I blurted.

"What are you talking about Carmen? This is the man I longed for. He is going to be my husband."

"Girl, I'm sorry, I was talking out loud yelling at this show on television. "Savannah the girls are up now, I have to go check on them, I'll call you back later okay, love you," I abruptly interrupted. I couldn't take it anymore.

"Alright girl cool; love you too."

I must be the worst friend ever. The first thing I wanted to do was eat, so I went to the kitchen and ate a bowl of cereal, and cooked pancakes, eggs, grits, and toast for breakfast that morning. Here was yet another thing to add to my eating binge. After the binges I always felt bad and regretted doing it, then at times I would also cry myself to sleep. This thing with food was like a bad disease. I prayed to God that when Savannah did find out the truth that she would forgive me. I hope she understands how I was between a rock and a hard place, and that the situation was out of my hands.

****

A few weeks after Savannah found out she was having a baby girl, she called me hysterical. I had no idea what was going on and tried to prepare myself for the worst. I drove so fast I was afraid I'd be stopped by the police. She was crying and wouldn't tell me what was wrong. So many other thoughts ran through my mind. Did she miscarry? Was something wrong with the baby? I tried to think positive, but all the negative thoughts continued to bombard my mind.

When I pulled up I jumped out of the car so fast I left my purse sitting on the front seat. I stopped in my tracks and turned to get my purse, but not before saying a quick prayer. "Please God, let Savannah and the baby be alright." When I arrived, she was on the phone screaming at the person on the other end I could hear her through the door. "Carmen is here. I'm ashamed to have to tell her this! I never saw this coming, but why shouldn't I have? My mother was right; no man is ever going to love me. Now my daughter's and my life is over. How could you do this? Lies! I don't believe you. I'll call you back!"

"Come in Carmen!"

"Hey Savannah, are you okay?"

"My whole life has changed in a day!"

"What are you talking about?"

Savannah laid her hand on my shoulder and continued to cry. "I want to tell you the events from today, but I don't even know where to start."

"Savannah, what happened? Try to calm down. You don't want to upset the baby. You have to pull yourself together."

"Carmen, please believe me I had no idea."

"Savannah I'm here for you no matter what."

As she spoke I was unable to look her in the face, only assuming the outcome from today. "Today was my regular appointment with Adriana to get my hair done. We were talking, and she started asking questions about the baby."

She paused for a moment to gather her thoughts. "So, you and Adriana were having a conversation, and?"

"I told her my boyfriend and I was having a girl, then she started asking me questions about him. She said she didn't realize that I was in a relationship."

Still looking down at the floor I lifted her head, so we could make eye contact. I needed her to know I cared. "Savannah breathe and take your time. I'm here for you."

She finally took a deep breath and continued. "So, I started telling her about Theodore, explaining the kind of car he drives, how we go out, and how happy we are. Then something happened. Something I wouldn't wish on my worst enemy."

"What Savannah?!"

"One of her clients' who was sitting two chairs down stood up and said I was lying, because the man I was describing was her husband! I thought there's no way he could be her husband."

"I told her she didn't know what she was talking about and must have mistaken him with someone else because he is supposed to be my husband one day!"

"Savannah, stop crying, I'm so sorry I…"

"No, wait Carmen, that's not even it! She pulled out a picture; of her, Theodore and their two kids, a son and a daughter. I was so hurt and embarrassed. She kept saying I was a liar and my baby wasn't her husband's. But worst of all, Adriana had the nerve to tell me I couldn't come back to her business after today with my drama."

"That's not right Savannah. She shouldn't have put you out. Especially, when she was the one who started the conversation."

"Carmen, this is hard. I don't know how I'm going to get through this."

"One day at a time, Savannah – one day at a time."

"I told Adriana I wasn't lying, and then I pulled out my cell phone and showed Theodore's wife our text messages. Especially the ones where we talked about the baby and him telling me how he loves us and one day we're going to be a family! I made sure she saw those messages."

"What did she say?"

"She knew then I was telling the truth. I told her I had no idea he was married, but she didn't believe me. She looked at me with so much rage and hurt in her eyes, then she turned to Adriana and told her she had to reschedule and left the shop."

"Why does this always happen to me!!! Even when I tried to get my own man, I find out he was never my man in the first place! That explains why he never spent the night. He claimed he was at the plant most of the time monitoring third shift because they messed up on some material."

"Savannah, I'm so sorry, I wanted to tell you. You don't deserve him; you are worth so much more than this."

"You knew! Carmen, you had me running around here with a married man and you knew the whole time!"

"Savannah, calm down, I…"

"Calm down!!! Carmen, that woman made a complete fool out of me!"

"Savannah, I promise I didn't know the whole time. I just found out at Adriana's party."

"What?!"

"Yeah, he and his wife were at the party."

"Well, that explains why he didn't want me to go. He didn't know Adriana did my hair, but he knew I was thinking about going to a party. He told me I needed to stay off my feet and that I should stay in and put my feet up."

"Savannah, when I saw him I wanted to ring his neck. He shook my hand and stared straight into my eyes as if we had never met! Like, he never had seen me before a day in his life."

"What?!"

"Devin kept telling me not to say anything because he was afraid to lose his job. I feel like such a bad friend; you have to believe I really wanted to tell you. If I would have told you, you wouldn't have had to go through this."

"I can't say I blame you Carmen, that's a lot. You were in a tough spot. I know you wanted to tell me, and I can imagine Devin stopping you if you tried. My life is playing out exactly how my mother said it would, and it's my own fault."

"Why would you say that, Savannah? That's not true, you have to believe different. Things will get better regardless of what this situation looks like. You must have faith to believe that."

"Well Carmen, if I wouldn't have..." she stopped herself before finishing her statement. "Savannah, I want to encourage you to develop a relationship with God. It will make a difference in your life. I'm changing for the better and so can you. At times things don't work out in life like we want it to because it's just not God's plan for our life. He has a better one for you.

"God? My life is too messed up for God."

"Girl, it doesn't matter how messed up you are, God can help you! After all He created you."

Would you like to come to church with me on Sunday?"

"I don't' know? Maybe God can help me and baby Hope. Her name has to be Hope, that's all I have to hold on to. I hope Theodore knows he will be in her life and take care of his child, married or not. Hope is going to have a relationship with her father, because that's something I never had."

"Savannah, this is something you're going to have to turn over to God. I have to go, but before I do I would like to pray. Is that alright?"

"Thanks Carmen, yes I would like that."

As I prayed I could tell Savannah felt better and became hopeful. "Carmen, what if my mom is wrong? What if God has a different say about my life? I have to become a better woman for Hope, she deserves it, and maybe I do too.

"Savannah, God does have a different say about your life."

Overcoming The Battle

Chapter Nine

Now that Savannah knew about Theodore, Devin and I was finally back on track, the way it was supposed to be. I could smell the flowers again and the eating binges were behind me. Well, maybe not completely. Devin and I had gotten into it about a month ago because I wouldn't have sex. That night I went to the club and ordered thirty lemon pepper chicken wings and ate all but five while driving home. Normally, I would have felt guilty, but it was either that or give in to Devin, and I was not about to break my vow again.

Since Devin had saved some money he decided it would be a good idea to take a family trip before the wedding. He thought it would be a good stress reliever with everything going on, especially planning the wedding, and his mother would be coming along. At first, I thought, maybe it would be a good trip for us and the twins, our little family. But then I thought it could be great also for Adriana and me to get a little closer. Besides, she could help me finalize my wedding plans with her great ideas.

While packing for the beach trip the girls and Devin went to the store for a few last minute things, and then had to pick up his mother. We were leaving in a few hours and I was really looking forward to our trip. About two weeks ago we finally came to an understanding concerning my commitment with God in regard to sex. I no longer had to sleep in my robe. He was now holding me at night, while we prayed for our future…well I prayed. I knew when I was praying too long, because he would say amen every couple of seconds. After prayer ended, the irritated look on his face said it all.

We were off to a good start, but I didn't want to be too pushy when it came to him going to church. About three weeks ago he and I were talking, and he told me that Adriana was married before. I was shocked as he told me the story about his ex-step-father, Pastor Caleb Newsome. I hadn't heard anything about a step-father until now, and was surprised that Adriana had been a preacher's wife.

"Carmen, I want to go to church, but the man, the only father I knew represented God so badly."

"Devin, everyone has made a mistake. I mean come on the man wasn't God himself."

"Mistake? You tell me how the pastor of the church can sleep with so many different women in the church. The lead singer was side-chick number one, but he ended up getting his secretary side chick, number two pregnant."

"Wow! I didn't know it was like that Devin."

"Yes, it was like that. He humiliated us and broke my mom's heart. Not to mention mine. I thought even though my real dad wasn't here, that I had a dad."

"Devin, I'm sorry I had no idea. But you have to give it another try. You're not going to church for your step-father, it's for you."

"Well, God needs to come down here himself and tell me to go before I go back into a church."

"Devin, I can only imagine how you feel. So, is this why we had to argue a month about getting married inside of a church?"

"Yeah, that's why. Thank my ex-stepfather the wolf dressed up in sheep clothing."

"But you can't let this stop you from ever returning to church. Okay, I get it, maybe not now, but someday you have too. He is still a man. And God is still God."

"I know your right. My mom has been trying to tell me the same thing. That was not God, but how people misrepresented God and mistreated people. She has forgiven that man, but I don't understand how."

"Because Devin, the forgiveness is not for your step-father, it's for your mother, and it's for you too. You have to release him; you can't continue to hold this anger toward him."

"Carmen, I really looked up to him, I loved him like he was my real dad. I didn't do anything to deserve this."

"No one said you did babe, and you didn't. You or, your mom didn't. But, it's important that you forgive him for you.

"Aight baby. I will work on it."

I wouldn't have ever imagined Adriana going through the trauma she experienced with her ex-husband. I had to hand it to her she was a strong woman. What she encountered has broken a lot of women. After talking to Devin, it made me think about Adriana actions toward me.

Maybe she was afraid of Devin getting hurt because of her own life experiences. It's as if she wanted to make sure she protected him, so he never has to experience being hurt again. I couldn't blame her, and it really made me forgive her for her actions and truly wanting to get to know more of her.

Although Adriana wanted to protect Devin, life is full of experiences and surprises, and as parents we want to protect our children from ever encountering anything harmful. I look back over my life and think about the girls, and how I fear them ever experiencing some of the things I did.

I've often asked myself how can I stop them from going down a path they shouldn't, but only the one God has for them? I realize more and more each day this is something I must pray about, and turn over to God daily. As long as I am training them up and instilling a great path for them to follow, I can't fear any trials they may experience in life.

Thankful

As I sat on the beach, I stared at the ocean,
Amazed at how the waves moved in motion,
What a beautiful sight it was to see,
All created by the one who rose from the grave for me.
God, I just want to say thank you.
Although, a lot of times you don't receive
the credit you're due.
I'm thankful for each day, it's refreshing and new.
So rain or shine,
I will always strive to put a smile on my face.
And be thankful for each day.
God each day is new with your mercy and grace.

Overcoming The Battle

Chapter Ten

It was a month before the wedding and I had spoken to all my family and friends as far as their roles for the wedding, everyone but one, my best friend Lloyd from Florida. We had been friends since we were fifteen. We were very close before I started dating Devin. Since Devin and I had been dating, we weren't as close, but we still spoke often, via text messages or social networking sites.

When we were in high school everyone assumed we were in a relationship and was keeping it a secret. So many girls in school liked Lloyd, but he refused to give them the time of day. They would cut their eyes and talk about me as we walked to our lockers or the cafeteria. I laughed at them and was always explaining to everyone that we were just friends.

When I first met Lloyd, we did try to do the boyfriend/girlfriend thing, but it didn't last a week. We were better at being friends. Thinking about our friendship, I decided to give him another call even though I had left him a few messages. I tapped my fingers on the table while listening to the phone ring, waiting for his answering machine again, but this time surprisingly he picked up. "Hello."

"Lloyd, I'm glad you decided to pick up. Finally, I've called you over a thousand times!"

"Carmen or should I say Mrs. Diaz? There you go being all sarcastic. Ha! Ha! Ha! But anyway, how are you?"

"Lloyd, that's not funny, I have been calling and leaving you messages. I hope you're still flying out for the wedding. I really want you to be a groomsman."

"Oh yeah, I just got my phone turned back on today. It still goes to voicemail when it's off."

"Oh, I didn't know what was going on."

"Yeah Carmen, this change is new and different for me, I used to make at least five hundred dollars a day and now I'm struggling to make that every two weeks. This fast food restaurant is not paying the bills. I'm hoping I get this Assistant Manager's position. At least it will be a little more money,"

"Lloyd, you have to believe your situation is going to get better. I know from the looks of things it seems like it won't, but you have to believe it will."

"My pastor Brian Richardson always says, "We must walk by faith and not by sight. Even though it may seem like things are the worst ever; change is possible and inevitable. And yes, it may be something new, but a change is going to keep you off the streets and out of jail!"

"I hear you Carmen. But church? Ha! I thought you stop going since you got away from your Grandma Ruth Anne," He giggled a little.

"Yes, I go to church at times. Devin's Aunt Isabel kept asking me, so I decided to go," I said not being completely honest.

It'll be nice when I get like Aunt Isabel. She's not afraid to talk about the goodness of the Lord, and how she feels about Him. She lets everyone see and know she loves

God and if they don't like it, then oh well, that was their problem not hers. On the other hand, I was too afraid of what people might think and didn't want to be called a "Jesus Freak."

"Cool, that's what's up. So, this wedding is still going to happen, huh?"

"Yes, it's still going to happen, Lloyd!"

"If it's happening, then yes you know I'm going to be there for you. I have to get the money, but don't worry about that, I'll make it happen."

"It's only a month away. I'm so glad you're coming to be a part of my big day."

A few months after Devin and I started dating, there were rumors that Lloyd walked in on Devin and his sister. Since then Lloyd said I could do better and I was settling. Devin convinced me that Lloyd was lying, and every time I tried to get a hold of Lisa, Lloyd's sister, she was nowhere to be found. But when I did see her I didn't know who to believe. I didn't want there to be a feud between my friend and my boyfriend, so I lied and told Lloyd we broke up. Most of the time, I was the type of person who had to see things with my own eyes to believe it.

"Lloyd, if you need any help with your flight, tux, or anything, just let me know. I'm willing to help you with what I can."

"Nah Carmen, this is your day, I'll be alright. I will be there, and I'll get everything I need."

"That's fine, just don't do anything illegal to get what you need, again I'm willing to help you. Be encouraged and know that things will get better and you will start to enjoy living life the legal way."

"I hope so, because these last ten months of living life the legal way has been a struggle!"

"You will, have faith I'll talk to you later, and see you soon."

"Alright Carmen, take care."

Chapter Eleven

It was two weeks before the wedding and I kept calling to make sure everything was in order: the cake, the venue, photographer and anything else I could think of. I continued to stress to everyone the importance of the RSVP. I warned them if they didn't RSVP, there would not be a place for them, and I wasn't joking.

I tried not to think negative and thought positive, everything had to be perfect. As soon as I thought of one thing going wrong a million other thoughts came to mind. This wedding was stressing me out, but more importantly I will be Mrs. Diaz, and that's all that matters.

I put in my two week's notice at the club and tonight was my last night. Henry was a little disappointed and only hopes to replace me with someone that can provide good service like no other. Today Henry asked me to come to the club about an hour earlier before it opened. He said if I did I could leave early, so I thought, *'sure.'* But with Devin working over tonight, I was thinking of staying until closing time since it was my last night.

When I walked inside the club it was pitch black. "What in the world? Was the utility bill not paid?"

I tripped and stumbled over a stool and before my face could hit the floor, Henry caught me. The lights were turned on and voices around me screamed, "SURPISE!!!"

"Henry, you did this for me?"

Henry had thrown a surprise party for me, which was shocking. There was food, gifts, and everyone that worked at the club from the bartenders, to the host and even the security guards were there. Henry always meant business. I was so used to him fussing and getting on everyone that I didn't think he had it in him to do something so emotional. "Carmen, wipe those tears. I'm going to miss you. This is a happy moment. Why wouldn't I do something for one of the best dog-gone bartender's ever?"

"I don't know Henry – no one has ever done anything like this for me. Thank you so much; you have no idea how much this means to me."

"Well, if you ever decide to come back to work, I hope you know the door is always open for you."

"Thanks Henry, but no thanks. I will be enjoying being Mrs. Diaz and a full-time stay-at-home mom for now."

"I know you will I just wanted to let you know. Enjoy, let me go handle something before we open."

"Congratulations Carmen!"

"Thanks Kelly, you make sure you hold it down at the bar."

"Girl, I have no choice, or daddy Henry will kill me if I don't."

"Y'all better not be laughing and talking about me. This is nice, but we have an hour until the club doors open. Let's clean up and get ready for business!" Henry yelled.

After the surprise party my decision was made to work all night. I texted Devin and told him I would be working all night and would see him in the morning. Now it was time for me to enjoy my last night working at the club with people that would be missed dearly.

The crowd was huge as usual, but I could spot that smile from anywhere. "Hello Carmen, how are you?"

There he was in his usual spot near the bar. "What can I get you to drink Chad?

"I heard tonight is your last night working here, I just wanted to tell you congratulations and I hope the best for you and your family."

"Awe, thanks Chad, that's so nice of you. Yes, tonight is my last night. What are you ordering, it's on me tonight?"

"For real, it's my lucky night then, but I'm good, again congratulations, and I guess good bye as well."

"I'll still be here in Houston; I'll see you around."

Chad got up, looked at me with those beautiful white teeth. "Well, take care beautiful."

"Goodnight Chad."

Glancing at the hundred dollar bill he had left, made me smile, thinking to myself, *'He is going to make his wife a very happy woman.'*

"Go ahead Carmen, it's your last night and you can leave."

"It's okay Henry, Devin is working over tonight, and my sister has the girls. I'm going to stay all night."

"No, you are not Carmen, go ahead, and I'm not taking no for an answer."

"Henry, it is only two-thirty, it is way too early, look at this crowd."

"Carmen, if you don't leave now I'm going to put you out," he said hugging me tightly. "I'm sure going to miss you, continue to keep that beautiful smile and great spirit of yours, you hear."

"I will Henry. You're a good person, not to mention a great business man."

"I will see you around."

Chapter Twelve

When I pulled into the drive way, I noticed Devin car, but it was only three o'clock in the morning, he must have gotten off early. I couldn't wait to tell him about Henry and the crew at the club throwing me a surprise party. In only two days we were going to get our marriage license. I couldn't wait until the night of our honeymoon to make love; Devin had been waiting so patiently.

Slowly opening the door and entering the house it was pitch black, but I could hear music playing from upstairs, which was weird since it was coming from our bedroom. As I walked up the stairs I knew it had been months since we had sex, but did he need it that badly he had resulted in going back to watching pornography?

I could hear moans coming from the bedroom. *'Wow he is really watching porn?'* As I opened the door the lights were off, but there were candles lit all around the room. It felt like my body or better yet, my entire life was a movie that was put on pause for a moment. I couldn't move and was in disbelief to what I saw.

My eyes had to have been lying to me. It looked just like Savannah from the back, with the dark curly hair that fell to her shoulders. She was going up and down on top of Devin as he caressed her back and kissed her. I could see her baby bump bouncing up and down on his stomach. "Devin, what the hell?!!!"

The woman turned around quickly. It was Tammy, Savannah's first cousin. They looked so much alike, they could have passed for twins. Tammy jumped off the bed and ran into the corner. I went charging after her and saw a vision of myself punching her face in over a hundred times until she stopped breathing. "Devin, get her! Get her! Devin, she is going to hurt our baby!!!"

"What did that trick say Devin?"

Cristal was telling the truth the whole time. It was never about her being jealous of Devin and our relationship. Cristal must have assumed that Savannah was my sister. She thought Tammy was Savannah. That explained why Cristal continued to say that she knew she was my sister, because we were together all the time.

Devin grabbed me when I went for Tammy. I literally felt sick. I fought and struggled to break from his grip. At the same time, I felt like throwing up. Devin grabbed me and laid me down on the bed. Even when I fought hard to get him off me, his grip became tighter. "How could I have been so stupid? After all the cheating, black eyes, broken arm, and two miscarriages, I still stayed with you. Devin, we are supposed to get married in two weeks! How could you do this to our family?"

I don't think Devin even thought about his actions before he did what he did. He never considered me or the twins. What Devin wanted, Devin was going to get, no matter who he hurt in the process. How could I love someone so selfish? "And that slut is having your baby?!! What the hell, Devin?!!! Boy and you in here with candles all lit up like you making love. Do you love her Devin?"

"Man come on Carmen, it ain't even like that?" He had a dumb look on his face.

From the looks of Tammy's belly, she was about six or seven months pregnant. I was for sure my heart dropped to my stomach and stop beating for a moment. I knew in the past Tammy had made passes towards Devin and couldn't be trusted. She was the type of woman you could only trust as far as you could see. She had even slept with some of the men Savannah had been with, so I knew her reputation.

Savannah told me Tammy was pregnant and was due about two weeks before her, but she didn't know who she was pregnant by. I never thought it could be Devin. Tammy was only twenty-two years old and was known as one of the biggest sluts in town. Now she was pregnant by my fiancé. My life, my whole world had fallen apart right before my eyes.

"Carmen, it's not what it seems like."

Did he really just say that? Was he stuck on stupid? "Let me make sure I understand. So, I walk into our bedroom in our home and you are screwing this slut in our bed, but it's not what it looks like?!!!"

If I could have gotten loose I would have punched him in his balls. Trust me; I would have made sure they didn't function again. "Are you hearing yourself right now?!!"

"Well, we don't know if the baby is mine. We have to do a DNA test when he comes."

"And that's supposed to make me feel better?" Tears started to roll down my face as I prayed to wake up from the nightmare I was having. *'This can't be real, I'm sleeping. This is a bad dream from wedding jitters,'* I thought. *'Devin and I are getting married in two weeks and things are going to be great. I will wake up from this any moment now.'*

I started to cry, and as much as I knew he didn't deserve anymore of my tears, I couldn't stop. I didn't want to cry, especially not in front of Tammy, but I couldn't hold them back. "*He,"* Devin, she's having your son?" The pain in my heart ached even more at the fact that Tammy may have been carrying Devin's son.

When I was pregnant with the twins, Devin and I hoped for a boy and a girl, but since we had two girls we always planned on having a son in the future. During the other two pregnancies we hoped for a boy, and then the miscarriages occurred before we could find out. "Carmen, I'm sorry, but I thought the wedding was off. Devin said it was over between you two." Her voice sounded as though I should have pity for her.

Tammy sat balled up sitting in the corner as if she was the victim in all of this. As if that would justify her being in bed with my fiancé. "Hoe, you have nothing to say to me! You knew we were still together. We both were together the other day when we saw you at the store. Get your stuff and get the hell out of my house while you still have a chance!"

Tammy approached us the other day at the store rubbing her stomach smiling very hard. She was telling it without telling then. Thoughts of killing her wouldn't stop playing in my head. Devin wasn't going to let me go. I couldn't get away regardless of how hard I tried.

Tammy slid on her clothes and grabbed her shoes. "For the record, yes, "he" is Devin's child! Devin and I have been on and off for a year!"

This was not another situation where I heard a rumor of him being with a female. My own saying, *"I would only believe it when I see it,"* hit me right in my face.

With my own eyes there it was, so I had to believe it. I heard Tammy running down the steps as fast as she could, slamming the door behind her. There wasn't another car in the yard, so she must have caught a ride. Maybe I can sweet talk Devin into letting me get up and I could still catch her to choke the life out of her.

Devin lifted me up from the bed and held me while I cried. I didn't want him holding me or touching on me, but I was lost in a sea of emotions. "Carmen, I'm sorry. I brought her over to talk about the baby, to see if she would get an abortion. This wasn't supposed to happen tonight. I know you've heard this a million times but, I'm sorry. I messed up and I'm going to do everything I can to make this right."

If I had a dollar for all the time he said, "I'm sorry," I would be a very wealthy woman. I got up from the bed and pulled my suitcase out of the closet, grabbed some of my clothes, and then went to the twin's room and grabbed their clothes. Devin followed me into the twin's bedroom, "Carmen, what are you doing?"

"What does it look like I'm doing? Devin, I'm seriously done. There is no way we can move on from this! You can go be with that hoe!"

"Don't start that packing mess again; we can fix this. We have to work this out. We are getting married in two weeks."

"Devin, you must be on crack, cocaine, meth and every other drug that exists if you think I'm still going to marry you. I have been to hell and back with you and I'm tired! I can't anymore. I'm not good enough for you – I get that now, so there is no need for me being here!"

"You know that's not true, you and the twins are the best thing that ever happened to me. You are good enough!"

I stopped packing for a moment and walked over to the dresser to gather some more items. I stood in front of the mirror and stared at myself. Looking at the woman in the mirror, she had no idea who she was. She had lost herself even more by putting so much love into a man that didn't deserve it.

Though I wasn't hungry, I could feel an eating binge coming on. In my mind I was already eating two cheeseburgers, fries, and a milkshake. As I looked at my features, they made me wonder what I could have fixed to make him love me more. "Carmen?" He interrupted my thoughts.

"What is it Devin? Am I not skinny enough? I told you I was going to lose some weight. Am I not pretty enough? I love you with everything in me!!!"

Sad thing was, after all these years, I don't believe he ever loved me. "Please help me understand what's wrong with me? If you would have talked to me and told me, I would have fixed it!"

Devin looked up at me all pitiful, like someone should feel sorry for him. "Nothing Carmen, it's nothing. Like I said, I messed up again, but I promise it won't happen again."

"You got that right," I went back to packing.

"Carmen, please, I'm sorry. We have to work this out. We have over two hundred guests coming for the wedding in two weeks."

Devin was more worried about getting married and the guest than coming to grips with the fact there was no longer going to be a wedding. He had so much pride and would be completely embarrassed if he had to tell his family the wedding was off. It was an event they had been looking forward to for the last seven months.

"Devin, are you serious? I'm not marrying you, go marry Tammy!!! That way you can still have your beloved wedding."

He finally put on his shorts, walked over to me and grabbed my arm. "We have spent too much money on this wedding. We are getting married!"

"Devin, we are not, you'd rather be with a woman the whole town has run through than be with someone committed to you and only you. You don't want a woman that loves you, now let me go!"

"Hell no, I won't let you go. We are still getting married," I tried to pull away from him, but he was not letting go. He wrapped his hands around my neck, and slammed me down on the bed. "Devin please, stop! You're hurting me!!!"

"If you dare try to leave, I will kill you. Do you understand? This wedding is still going to happen, so go put those clothes back in the drawers."

"Devin, you're hurting me, I can't breathe."

"I said, do you understand, Carmen? We are going to work this out and this wedding is still going to happen."

"Yes Devin, I understand," I cried. Tears rolled down my face and I could taste the salt on my lips. I was so scared. This time I believed he could get angry enough to actually kill me. I had never seen that look in his eyes before. He grabbed me and forced me to lie in the bed with him and held me in his arms and rocked back and forth. "Don't worry baby, everything is going to be alright."

Fifteen minutes later I pretended to be asleep. Once I was sure he was sound asleep I could slide from his grip. Quickly, I grabbed my bags and ran down the stairs, got into the car and peeled out of the driveway. I drove away from our home with a heavy heart. Nothing could have prepared me for what I had just encountered.

Immediately, I called Charlotte and told her what happened. But I had to call her three times before she picked up. It was almost five o'clock in the morning, so I'm sure she was sound asleep. "Hello," she said in a sleepy voice.

"Charlotte, I'm sorry I woke you up, but I'm on my way over!"

"Carmen what's wrong?"

"The wedding is off! I will tell you about it when I get there. I hope you don't mind the girls and me moving in. I'm leaving him for good this time."

"Sure Carmen, just come and be careful. You know I got you."

"Okay, I will see you in a minute." Hanging up the phone, I looked out of the rear-view mirror at the house I would never return to.

When I called to check our account, the balance was only two dollars. I knew Devin was paying the expenses for the wedding, but I was sure the balance would have been more than two dollars. What was he doing with all his money? Maybe he was putting it aside for his new baby.

It didn't matter what he did with the money. I knew the overdraft protection would cover the amount from my transaction, so I filled up my car with gas. Devin was going to be pissed, but I could care less. He was probably going to cancel my bank card or even close the account to get back at me.

****

I wasn't sure how much longer we were going to be able to stay at Charlotte's. Devin was riding by her apartment every night. He would even hide out in the parking lot, hoping he would catch me coming out of the door. Then there were times when I'd catch him walking around the apartment building.

Charlotte's boyfriend Phillip said he didn't mind us being there, but I knew he was a little irritated with the drama being brought to his home. Devin was constantly calling and texting my phone every five minutes. He couldn't have been working because he wouldn't have had the time to do all the stalking he was doing.

Our situation was really starting to get to the girls. They missed their father, but they were too young to understand what was going on. Every morning they woke with, "Mommy when are we going home, I miss daddy?" Unfortunately, I didn't have an answer.

The wedding was nine days away and I had a decision to make. All our family and friends were expecting a wedding. I don't know why, but I never notified any of them of the cancellation.

Devin told Adriana I left, and of course she asked me what I had done. Looks like her old feelings towards me were back. I'm not sure if anything about her had really changed. And to think, I was starting to like her.

Now I didn't have a home, a job, or any money. I had put all my trust into Devin once again and he had everything taken from me. Then I started to think maybe Devin and I could get counseling? What if Tammy's baby wasn't his child? I would be letting her win if I decided not to marry him. Especially my family, they were probably taking bets to see if the wedding would happen or not.

I was so stressed and depressed, and hadn't had anything to eat in the five days, which was a surprise. This was definitely a first. At night I couldn't sleep. My overwhelming thoughts were consumed by the strange voices that filled my head. "Shut up! Please, shut up! Get out of my head," I'd cry.

"You were so bad he went and knocked someone else up. You should have been having sex with him. You call yourself trying to make a vow to God. Well, thank your God for the fact that you ruined your family. And you know you're too ugly for someone to love you."

"God, please make them go away, please!" I cried and prayed until the thoughts left my mind. What if we could work it out? I just needed to work on some things. If I continued to lose weight, and quit my eating binges I could make Devin love me and only me. There wouldn't be any more cheating. And if I stop nagging and complaining about everything the hitting would stop as well. I should have taken better care of myself. This is really all my fault. Finally, my decision was made. It was time for me to get my belongings and the girls and go back home.

Neither Charlotte nor Savannah was going to be happy about my decision, especially, Savannah. When I told her what happened, she said, "He doesn't deserve you Carmen. I hope you are really done with him this time. You are worth more than that. Let him be with that whore. I know she's my cousin, but she's a whore – they deserve each other."

What Savannah didn't know was I was at my wits end and had to do what I had to do. Besides, where else was I going to go? We couldn't continue to live with Charlotte and Phillip forever. Devin was all I knew. I couldn't sleep, eat, and sometimes felt like I couldn't breathe without him. If we try to work things out they have to get better.

Maybe I will work harder on my faith. I hadn't been praying lately like I should have. I know things will turn around for me and Devin real soon. Now I have to prepare to get married in nine days. But the hard part was getting past Charlotte. "Carmen where do you think you are going?" She said running to the door blocking me from leaving.

"Charlotte, please move out of the way. Everything is going to be okay. You'll see."

"No, I'm not moving anywhere!"

"Charlotte, I'm going back home to the man that's going to be my husband. The girls are missing their father like crazy. It's not fair that I continue to keep them from him."

"What's not fair is that I'm afraid I will be burying my sister and my nieces will grow up without their mother. Carmen, you are smart, you're beautiful, and you know you can do so much better than this. Why do you want to go back to him anyway?"

"I love him, and we have children together. I believe things will get better."

"Oh, did you quickly forget that fast how you were not going to be the only one with children by Devin? Carmen, you have been saying things will get better since you were in college. He hit you four months after you were in a relationship with him. And let's not forget, when he first cheated on you with Lloyd's sister only a few months after you started dating him. Everybody knows Devin slept with Lisa."

'Wow! Even my sister knew the truth.'

"Do you want to die?!" Tears were now rolling down Charlotte's face as she begged me not to leave. "My nieces should not have to see their mother going through this! What do you think you are showing them? You're telling them it's okay for a man to treat them the way their daddy treats you. That it's okay for a man to hit on them whenever he feels like it. He can talk to you anyway and treat you like a piece of crap."

"Grandma always told us how we should be treated by a man. She constantly drilled in our heads when daddy hit mama that it was wrong. She said that wasn't love and no way for a man to treat a woman!"

Seeing her cry caused me to start crying. I understood what Charlotte was saying, but I was so comfortable with Devin. We had too much history to just end it. There may have been more bad than good, but I felt lifeless without him and I wanted my kids to grow up with both parents.

"Charlotte, please don't cry. I have to go, please let me and the girls leave. I hope you will understand one day."

Charlotte stood for a moment staring at me with a mad, disgusted look on her face. "You know what? It doesn't matter what I say, he has you, so brain washed you can't even see that it could cost you your life."

Charlotte moved out of the way, and let us leave. "I'm sorry Charlotte, pray and trust that everything will get better for us."

"I'm sorry too. I will prepare to bury my sister and raise my nieces as my own." Her statement made me feel really low, but I couldn't make myself change my mind. I really believed that we were going to work it out and get married in nine days.

I was on my way out of Charlotte's apartment until my phone started ringing. I was sure it was Devin calling again. Now I could let him know that the girls and I were on our way home. As I reached for my phone I looked on the Caller ID and saw that it was Aunt Isabel.

When I saw her name, I dried my face and made sure I didn't sound upset when I answered. Aunt Isabel always called to check on us. She may not even know what happened between me and Devin. Since the time she walked in on Devin hitting me, she checked on me and the girls weekly. "Hello."

"Carmen, how are you?"

"Hey Aunt Isabel, I'm good, and you?"

"I'm fine, but if you are good why did my sister call me saying that you had left Devin? I knew I couldn't get the truth out of her, so I decided to call to see what's going on. Adriana said you threatened to cancel the wedding."

I should have known Devin ran to his mother to tell her about our problems, as usual. Who knows what story he had told her? It was always far from the truth. "Yes, I did leave for a few days, but the twins and I were actually about to go back home. Devin and I are going to work everything out."

"Carmen, what happened this time? Why do you keep putting yourself through this? Adriana said you left because of the baby, but why would you leave if you already knew?"

"Aunt Isabel, what do you mean? I found out about the baby the other night when I walked in on him screwing her in our bed."

"Wait a minute, Aunt Isabel you already knew Tammy was pregnant?"

"Oh, my goodness Senorita, I thought you already knew. I'm so sorry. Adriana told me about a week before Devin proposed to you. That's why I asked you if everything was okay the day he proposed. I felt it in my spirit things were not going well, but when you said they were, I decided to leave it alone and not meddle."

That explained why Devin purchased the ring a week prior to when he proposed. Devin had found out Tammy was pregnant, so he thought it would be better to propose and we go ahead and get married before the baby came. Now it all made sense.

"The truth is, Aunt Isabel, Devin hit me the day before he proposed and before I left he choked me and told me he would kill me if I didn't marry him."

"I should have known things were not as great as you said they were – I knew it."

"Aunt Isabel, once Devin gets help, I'm sure he will change."

"Carmen, you talk like it's that easy. But what if he doesn't? And then it will be too late. Can I meet you and the girls somewhere? I want to show you something. Besides, I would love to see you and my beautiful nieces. What if we meet at a gas station or something?"

"Okay, give me about twenty minutes. How about we meet on Valentine Blvd. at the donut and coffee shop?"

"Sounds great, see you guys soon."

"Charlotte, that was Aunt Isabel, I'm going to meet with her, and then I will call you once we're back at home." We exchanged our goodbyes, but I didn't know that would be the last time I would see my sister for a while.

Chapter Thirteen

About five minutes before arriving at the gas station Aunt Isabel called to let us know where she was sitting. When we got there, she had already ordered donuts and coffee. As soon as we approached the booth she got up and gave us hugs and kisses. Mackenzie and Taylor were excited to see her, but even happier to see the donuts she had waiting for them.

"Come Carmen, sit, I want to share something with you." She reached for her purse and pulled out a package. Inside were pictures. The first picture was of a young Hispanic couple. "This is a nice-looking couple Aunt Isabel, but who is it?"

"That's Ricardo and me. We dated for two years and I loved him more than life itself."

"That's you!? I had no idea."

"Yes Carmen, that's me when I was twenty-four years old. It was just a few months before I became pregnant with our daughter Alexandria."

"Aunt Isabel, you look so different. "Aunt Isabel looked at me and smiled, then pulled out another picture. She took a sip of her coffee as I stared at the next picture in disbelief. "That's me Carmen, lying on my death bed."

I scratched my head as I studied the picture. "Well, that's what the doctors said. They expected me to die along with the child I was carrying, but what an awesome God we serve. He always has the last say, and not man," she said smiling.

I was in total shock, and couldn't believe it was Aunt Isabel in the picture. Her face was covered completely with bandages, while tubes ran from her nose. She was even on a ventilator.

"Carmen, I was so in love with Ricardo I took anything. The very first time he hit me, he said it would never happen again, that was a lie," she said while shaking her head. "I was like you Senorita, believing he was going to change. I too had low self-esteem. In that picture I had a total of fifty-six stab wounds all over my body."

"Huh, low self-esteem. Aunt Isabel as beautiful as you are, I can't see you having low self-esteem."

"Yes Carmen, only a woman with low self-esteem and no self-worth would allow herself to go through an abusive relationship. Some women are in such deep denial they don't even realize it. See, a woman who loves herself, and knows her worth would not allow herself to go through such an ordeal."

"I don't know how to love myself though," I explained to Aunt Isabel as tears formed in my eyes.

"It's okay, don't cry, I understand all too well. I let a man destroy me from the inside of my spirit to the outside of my body. I had been overweight for years and had an eating disorder. The eating disorder was from depression from being bullied and picked on, being sexually assaulted as a child, and other obstacles.

So, when Ricardo came into my life and told me he loved me, I was all in. Even though he treated me like crap after only a few months into the relationship I allowed it because he was the first man to really love me for me, or so I thought. I lost myself loving him, hoping he would change. It wasn't until I almost died, and it's only by the grace of God that I'm still here today."

"Did he just decide to go crazy one day, what happened?"

"It was a beautiful summer day when Ricardo came home while I was preparing to cook his favorite meal. He came in the house cursing and accusing me of cheating. He said he heard I was at the store with some guy earlier that day."

"Carmen, I hadn't been out of the house all day, because I was planning something special to show him how much I loved him. I was always thinking of ideas to make him happier."

Aunt Isabel watched me as I continued to look at the pictures, with tears streaming from my face. "Does that sound like someone you know?" She asked.

Still looking at the picture, I shook my head, "Yes."

"On the fourth day in the hospital, God worked a healing miracle. Adriana had been praying for me, because even if I was awakened I wouldn't have been praying for myself. My vitals had gone back to normal, so they went from expecting me to die the day before; to me and my baby surviving. They said we would live, and not die."

"Alexandria is my miracle baby. The doctors always told me because of my complicated menstrual cycles it would be impossible for me to carry a child to full term or even conceive a child for that matter. But I tell you, with God nothing is impossible."

Ricardo committed suicide two days later and was found dead inside of his car in Louisiana."

I couldn't believe what I was hearing. "Are you serious?" I knew she was, but it was just unbelievable.

"After several operations and plastic surgeries, no one would ever know that's me in this picture," she continued.

"Aunt Isabel, I cannot believe you survived something so horrible."

"Carmen, that's why I praise God the way I do. I love God so much and serve Him the way I do, because of who HE is! I know He saved my life. Before I went through the ordeal with Ricardo I used to be an atheist?"

"Aunt Isabel, I find that hard to believe."

"Well it's true. I said with all I went through as a child that there was no way there was a God. But there is evil in this world and the bible speaks about it. However, that's another topic for later. Silly me, I guess God said He was going to prove to me one way or the other that He was real."

"Wow."

"Carmen, Adriana was at the funeral home picking out my casket and preparing funeral arrangements when she received a call from the hospital that I was going to live. After being released from the hospital, I decided to go to counseling for my eating disorder. It was something I had to do. I carried that weight for years and battled with loving me."

Aunt Isabel's words penetrated me as she spoke. I would have never thought we struggled with the same demons. As she spoke I was speechless. "Carmen, I began a relationship with God and started to get to know who I was, discovering my worth, and started loving me, flaws and all. I started to pray and tell God the type of man I desired in my life, according to His will. When I met Victor, God confirmed several times that he was sent by Him. We love one another and make sure we keep God first in our marriage."

"That's amazing."

"Honey, God is AMAZING! Now I volunteer at different women's shelters sharing my story and inspiring other women who were or are being abused. I was very blessed to never have had to work after meeting Victor. I love to volunteer, and I know it's what God designed me to do. I'm very passionate about it. It's my reason for living, my purpose. I've seen women lives change when they discover who they really are and who God created them to be. The women start loving themselves and refuse to be treated any type of way by a man or anyone else for that matter. It gives me so much joy.

"So, what's your story Carmen? Do you know who you are?"

I heard her, but my mind was already made up. "Aunt Isabel, I already told Devin we're coming home, he's waiting on us. Besides, I have no money, and no place to stay."

Aunt Isabel reached inside her purse and handed me a credit card. "Here Carmen, take this and leave. It has a balance of a thousand dollars on it. Max it out if you need to. I will let Victor know, I'm sure he will understand." Aunt Isabel stared me in my eyes as a tear rolled down her face. "Carmen, I'm trying to save your life."

When she got up from the booth the girls and I followed behind her, but before getting into the car she gave us a hug and kiss. "I love you, y'all, be careful."

I pulled out of the coffee shop and stopped at the red light. I understood what she was saying, but I turned the car and made a left determined to go home to Devin. *'He has to change,'* I thought. The girls were in the back seat talking, then Mackenzie asked, "Mommy, why did Aunt Charlotte say that?"

"What do you mean? What did she say?"

Mackenzie had a worried look on her face. "When we left, Aunt Charlotte said do you want to die? Why did she ask you that? Are you going to die Mommy?"

"No baby, I'm not going to die."

I quickly made a U-turn in the middle of the road. I drove through three red lights, and after the fourth light I took a right turn and merged onto I-45 North and told the girls we were going for a long ride and would make a few stops on the way. I turned on some music to calm my nerves while preparing for our fifteen-hour drive to Tampa, Florida.

Lust or Love?

What is Lust?
What is Love?
Knowing the difference is a must.
He cheats on her, beats on her, and tells her lies after lies.
She's all confused feeling misused and abused.
Not understanding a thing, he does,
At times it was really bad,
She feared he would be the reason she died.
She knew she had to end it for her life depended.
Even though he kicked her around like dust,
He really thought he loved her, but it was Lust.
Every night she got on her knees to pray,
She asked God, "Why does it have to be this way?"
Thinking she would never find love one day?
She never knew all the love she needed was always there.
Just waiting for her to open her heart and let him in.
As years went by the Lord sent her a husband.
He was a God fearing man that treated her like she was his Queen.
Then she understood why she went through that bad relationship.
God explained to her, that no one could show love or love without loving Him first.

Overcoming The Battle

Chapter Fourteen

It had been six months since we had moved back to Florida. The transition of the move was taking some time, especially for the girls. They were continuing to ask where their father was and when we were going back home. They wanted to see their grandmother as well. I had to explain to them daily this was our new home now.

Since I'd been in Florida I had lost a total of thirty pounds, but from time to time fought having an eating binge moment. I started carefully watching the foods my body was taking in.

It was good to be back at home near family and friends. Lloyd had gotten me a position at Mega Burgers & Fries, where he was an Assistant Manager. Thankfully he didn't have any comments about the wedding. He said he could look in my eyes and tell I was hurting.

About a day after I got to Florida, I started calling family and friends, telling them that the wedding was cancelled. So many of them were upset because they had already purchased flights. I thought I would never hear the end of it. Especially, the wedding party, but I promised once I'm back on my feet they would be reimbursed.

It seemed as though I was giving apologies a thousand times a day. My family was making bets the wedding wouldn't happen. Uncle James had lost $200 to my father. He was so confident I would marry Devin regardless. My Uncle James even believed I was still moving back to Texas, after I had driven all the way to Florida. He continued to say, "You know that girl is not going to leave that boy alone. It's like he done put some type of voodoo or witchcraft on her, she ain't going nowhere. That boy has done everything a person could think of to her and she still stayed with him. She might as well marry him; he done got away with everything but murder."

My dad was against us getting married. As a matter of fact, Pretty Boy was against us dating. He always said he picked up a bad vibe from Devin. How ironic was it for someone to say they picked up a bad vibe from someone who portrayed the same habits from their past life? But Pretty Boy didn't see his identical faults in Devin.

Devin was for sure that I was coming back to Texas. He told me he thought of committing suicide if I didn't come home, but his social network pictures looked as though his life couldn't have been better. It turned out Tammy's child was his son. They had a blood test two weeks after the baby was born. Devin couldn't deny him if he wanted to. Baby boy was identical to Devin, and looked like the twins when they were babies. Savannah had texted me a picture of the baby.

"Hey Carmen, how are you?"

"Hey Savannah, I'm good and you?"

"I'm great, did you get that picture I texted you?"

"Yes, I got it."

"Man doesn't he look just like Devin?" And Tammy said he was even there when she had the baby.

"Yes, there is no denying him. It still hurts but hey, it is what it is. Sad, he was denying his own flesh and blood."

"I'm sorry Carmen. But I thank God, he saved you from making the biggest mistake of your life and marrying him. You deserve so much better."

"I know. Hey everything gets better with time, right?"

"Yes, it does and in due time when the amazing man comes along who is for you, you will be shouting "Thank You Jesus! Hallelujah!! And glad that Devin was not the one!" she laughed.

She put a slight smile on my face. "How is my beautiful god-daughter doing?"

"Girl is getting big and keeping me busy. I'm so in love with her Carmen."

"And what about her father?"

"Hmmmm...Let's see. So, he thought I was going to continue to have sex with him and believe the "*I'm going to leave my wife for you lie.*"

"Savannah did you continue having sex with him?"

"Carmen I'm not going to lie, I let him fool me and did it a few times, but I stopped all of that completely right before Hope was born."

"Well good for you. Ask God to forgive you and keep on moving."

"Girl that is exactly what I did. Theodore can continue being the father he is, and I must admit he is a good father to Hope. Keep paying his $4,000.00 a month in child support and keep it moving!"

"I know that's right Savannah. At least you are getting help financially."

"Now, Devin knows he is wrong for that."

"His day will come. Oh, what about his wife, how is she acting."

"They are still together, dealing with it I guess. I told Theodore as long as she respects our child there wouldn't be an issue."

"Okay that's good. God will send the right man for you too when the time comes."

"Amen to that!"

"I've started a new journey Carmen and decided to start going to counseling."

"For real? Because of Theodore."

"Well it goes back further than Theodore and the reason why my mother and I don't have a relationship."

"Huh?"

"Carmen when I was fifteen years old my mother came home early from work one day and walked in on me having sex with my step dad, the last one. He raped me for year, but she didn't believe me."

"What?! Savannah I'm so sorry to hear that."

"She said it would be the reason I would never have a man of my own, because I messed with her man."

"That's crazy. How in the world would your own mother not believe you?"

"It's okay. I had to realize I had to get to the root of my issues from not growing up with my father and being raped. I couldn't continue having sex with these men thinking that would solve my issues. It was pure self-destruction."

"Are you serious, she didn't believe you?!"

"Nope! She said I came onto him. Kicked him out, and divorced him. And she told me not to mention it to anyone. My family still doesn't know till this day."

"Again Savannah, I'm so sorry that happened to you."

"It's time for me to forgive and heal so I can be the mother I need to be for Hope, more importantly the woman God created me to be."

Since my leaving, she had become a member at Still Waters Outreach Church and was working daily on her relationship with God. I was grateful that she continued to share Pastor's messages with me. If only I had a reliable laptop, it would allow me to watch services online. I was rarely reading my Bible and forgot to pray from time to time. My life had been turned upside down and I didn't know how God could let me go back to living, barely having any money and struggling to pay bills.

Devin was so mad when we left he refused to send me any money to help with the girls. He always threatened coming to Florida to get them. I believe he thought since he wasn't sending any money we would eventually come back to Texas. Even though he didn't help with the girls, I still allowed them to speak to him when he called and allowed them to call him. I was never going to be so bitter and interfere with him having a relationship with our daughters.

I was doing everything to forgive Devin, but it was hard. For some reason I thought it would make me feel better. I thought back to one of Pastor Brian's messages on un-forgiveness. He spoke about holding on and not forgiving causes a constant turmoil within and most times we can't pinpoint that it's from not forgiving others or ourselves. Things are supposed to get better with time, but I struggled with my faith at times and couldn't see the better to come. The first four months, the girls and I lived with my grandmother. Staying with her allowed me to save a little money while working at Mega Burgers & Fries. I never imagined working at a fast food restaurant, flipping greasy burgers, mopping floors, cleaning restrooms, and dealing with customers with bad attitudes, but I had to do it. Life has a funny way of turning, but I told myself it was temporary.

There I was living back in Florida at Smithstone James Housing where I grew up. I was so glad they were remodeled. Moving was not a choice since about twenty people was living at my grandmother Ruth Anne's house. Well not twenty people literally, but it felt like it. There was also my younger sister Chasity, Uncle James, and his three children living there as well. It was too many people living in her three-bedroom house.

The girls and I pretty much stayed to ourselves at the apartments. There was a new playground area built when they remodeled, so we hung out there. They had nice ceiling fans in every room, new marble counter tops in the kitchen, new refrigerators and microwaves. The waiting list was very long for a two or three-bedroom apartment, so the girls and I moved into a one-bed room. Living there brought back too many memories.

Now don't get me wrong, the remodeling was nice, but it was the same atmosphere where the people still carried the same habits and mindsets. I always looked at living there, along with my job as my temporary situation and tried not to get comfortable. Pastor Brian said, "*You have to look at your situation like you want it to change. Walk by Faith, not by sight. Hope and believe your situation will change.*"

An old friend of mine who went to school with me was the Assistant Manager at Smithstone James and although the waiting list was over a year long, she could pull some strings. Thanks to her, we could get into an apartment only a month after filling out the application. I had to make the best out my situation. It may not have been where I wanted to be, but I was grateful for our place. Being there was bittersweet and now I was forced to deal with the demons of my past.

Overcoming The Battle

Chapter Fifteen

If I had to work another hour taking orders or flipping burgers, I was going to lose it. I had already worked over twelve hours and I was exhausted. Opening at four in the morning was wearing me out. Now, here it was almost five o'clock in the evening and I was still there. It was a good thing my grandmother didn't mind me working long hours. She knew I was trying to make a better life for the girls. Grandma Ruth Anne being on disability was a blessing, because I didn't have to put the girls inside of a daycare.

Although I was grateful for the position, it was a little irritating at times having Lloyd as my manager. He was demanding and bossy, or maybe I didn't like being told what to do by my best friend. He would always tell me he was only doing his job, not to take it personal. He was right, but I still didn't like it.

No matter how many hours I worked, the one thing I dreaded was pulling up to her house and seeing Seth's car in the driveway. *'Does he ever go home?*

Seth Washington was my baby sister Chasity's boyfriend. After Charlotte moved to Texas to help with the girls, I tried to get Chasity to come with her, but she wouldn't. At the time Chasity was in love with her ex Daniel. When Seth came along there was no way she was going to move.

Chasity was young, and gorgeous with a bachelor's degree in accounting. After she got her degree she couldn't see leaving Florida, there was too much money to be made.

Although neither one of us had the best relationship with Pretty Boy, Chasity was the youngest and his favorite. I believed she always saw him how she wanted to see him. She always took up for him regardless of the situation. That's one of the reasons why she is still living with grandmother. Not because she couldn't afford it, but she like her father liked to party and shop. How can an accountant, who is single, not handle their own finances? I thought to myself at times.

I didn't know much about Seth, only what others said. He has six kids and all but two have a different mother. It wasn't the fact that he had six children. It was the fact that Mr. Washington couldn't possibly be spending any time with his kids, because he was always on my grandmother's couch. He didn't even seem like Chasity's type. She never liked guys who walked around with their boxers showing, and pants down to their ankles.

Chasity was always into the clean cut, suit wearing type of guys. Seth was different from her last boyfriend Daniel, who was a good guy. They dated for years, then suddenly Chasity said things were no longer working out and ended it. Now she's lowered her standards to someone who wasn't worth her time. I'm still trying to figure out what she sees in him.

I walked into Grandmother's house and there was Seth on her couch like he lived there. "Grandma thank you so much for watching the girls," rolling my eyes at Seth.

"That was a good ole tight hug Shuga; you know it's not a problem"

My grandmother was a beautiful lady. She was very tall, especially for a woman, that's where my father got his height from. Her hair was sandy brown curly with only a few streaks of gray, and her hazel eyes were the same as mine.

Being the oldest of the three, Grandmother was always closer to me than Charlotte and Chasity. I really missed those days when we used to sit and talk. My love for her was more than anyone could ever imagine. She would give my sisters and me the world if she could.

Grandma always helped our mother out anytime she needed her to babysit, and treated her as if she was her daughter. When Pretty Boy messed up on the bills and we were evicted she let us live with her until my mom found a place. She didn't allow Pretty Boy to come because she said it was his fault that we had nowhere to go. That was one thing about my grandmother, wrong was wrong and right was right. It did not matter who you were, family or strangers.

My mother and Pretty Boy finally separated after we became homeless. It was due to my dad's drug addiction that we ended up having no place to live. My grandmother helped us out a lot, making sure we had food on the table and a roof over our heads. Now, it's not like we lived in the nicest or biggest home at grandmother's house, but it was home.

After growing up in an environment like that, I always wanted a better life. Pretty Boy was too busy in the streets and sleeping in somebody else's bed. He always made sure he had somewhere to stay, while we were left stranded.

As my grandmother walked towards the kitchen it reminded me of those times. "Baby, stop thanking me for watching these children, you know I don't mind. You're doing all you can to take care of these girls, by yourself," she emphasized.

"I'll help you in any way I can. But, it would be nice if that father of theirs helped in some type of way. He could send you some money or something. I don't know what's wrong with these boys. They can make these babies and not take care of them. Ooh child, if he doesn't remind me of your father," she said looking at Seth.

I guess that was his que. Chasity was taking a shower and he was waiting on her to get out, but the atmosphere started to get too heated for him. "Alright Mrs. Wilson, I'll see you later. Can you tell Chasity I'll be back around eight to pick her up?"

Grandma threw her hand up in the air and said, "Yes," like, "okay – whatever boy."

I couldn't help but laugh at how her comment quickly ran him off. She was going to say how she felt, when she wanted, regardless of how it made the other person feel. "These men are not taking care of their kids and I don't condone it. But, wait a minute now, because you ladies aren't all that innocent. I don't understand this commitment without a commitment to these men."

'This is going to hurt.'

"Why are you young girls so quick to submit to these men who are not even your husband's? It doesn't make sense to me? Marriage is nowhere in the picture, but you're steady having these babies, cooking, cleaning, paying his bills, and making sure he has a place to lay his head."

'She is so right.'

"Back in my day, we had a lot of respect for marriage. Men knew they had to marry us before they were going to get anything in our pants or have us playing "*wifey.*" Yes, y'all love saying, "I'm his wifey." To my knowledge if you're not married you are SINGLE! They must have changed something I don't know about. So, you can be married without being married now, huh? I want y'all to hush with that mess, talking about "I'm wifey." It just makes me mad!"

"Too many men feel like and say, "Why buy the whole cow when you can get the milk for free." If you women today were more confident, and secure I don't think y'all would take half of the crap these men giving y'all."

Grandma was right. I never looked at it that way, but started to have a different view once I restarted my relationship with God. I understood where she was coming from, but when I mentioned it to some of my friends, they saw it differently. They were so confident that their child's father was going to marry them one day. Even though there was no ring, or talks of marriage, they always said they knew it would happen.

"I know Grandma, but my thinking is different now. By the grace of God, I'm not having sex again until I'm married."

"Well praise the Lord! I hope you 're right. If any of these boys try to come at you without a ring…" She had to stop a moment and catch her breath. "Listen carefully," Grandma said staring me right between the eyes. "You better take a Bible, throw it between your legs and tell them your body is a temple," she said laughing.

I was cracking up picturing me putting a Bible in between my legs to keep from having sex. "Speaking of men Butterball, have you talked to your father?"

She must have had something to gossip about, because she had that look. "No ma'am, not lately."

"Oh, well let me tell you." Those were always the words she said before she began to tell a juicy story.

"You know Grandma, I called him because I hadn't heard from him in weeks, and that's not normal. Not to mention, when I did talk to him we only spoke for maybe two minutes. He rushed me off the phone saying he was tied up doing something."

"Butterball, he been running back and forth up the road to Tennessee to see about your Uncle Greg. I think something is going on with him," she said whispering as if we weren't the only two sitting at the kitchen table.

"What do you mean Grandma? You know Pretty Boy. It's probably nothing."

"Oh, it's something, I know it is, but your daddy won't tell me," Grandmother said pointing her index finger. "Watch what I tell you, oh it's something."

"Grandma, I'm sure it's nothing. What did you cook for dinner?" Trying to change the subject, I wasn't in the mood to talk about Pretty Boy.

"Oh baby, I cooked some pork chops, pinto beans and collards. The girls ate, now they're taking a nap. Go ahead and help yourself."

I got up from the table and headed towards the cabinet to retrieve a dish to fix a plate while she continued. "That ole step-mother of yours is so worrisome, you know. She keeps calling, coming over, and constantly asking me why your father keeps going to Tennessee. I try not to answer the door most of the time, but one of your cousins always let her in. Shoot, I told her she needs to get a hobby instead of stressing over that boy!"

"Carmen, I don't understand how such a beautiful lady so successful would be worried about a man who treats her the way he does. I know that's my son, but I'm gon'...Let me say – what it is you young people say today? I'm just gone keep it real," she laughed.

"Grandma, you are silly."

"I'm going to find out. I'm going to find out real soon. I can feel it, something ain't right."

"Grandma, I'm going to wrap my plate up and take it home with me instead. Let me go speak to Chasity and wake the girls up so that we can leave," I said in a tone that sounded as though I didn't want to be bothered.

I wasn't in the mood to discuss my father or Uncle Greg. "Carmen, is everything okay baby?" Grandmother asked in a very concerned voice.

"Yes ma'am, I'm just tired. I need some rest."

"Okay, well go ahead so you can get home and get some rest."

"Taylor, wake up baby. Mackenzie, mommy is here, come on, wake up girls so we can go home."

"Mommy, I miss daddy. When are we going home? I wanna go home with daddy."

"Baby, stop crying it's okay. After you get home, you can take a bath, and then I will let you call your daddy."

"Okay mommy." My heart ached like never before. It was times like these that pissed me off thinking about what Devin had done to our family. "Mommy!"

"Yes, Taylor baby, I see you woke now"

"Let's go mommy, is it time to go home?"

"Yes baby, we are going home."

"Yay, I get to see daddy!" Taylor said, somewhat excited, but also sleepy.

"Mackenzie and Taylor, girls this is home. Florida is home. Maybe I can talk to your dad to see what we can do about you seeing him soon, okay."

"No mommy, I want daddy now!" Taylor screamed. As I tried to hug and soothe her, she pulled away. She was mad at me because she couldn't see her father. As if it were my fault we weren't together.

I sat watching my daughters and how the situation was affecting them. I could see Chasity from the corner of my eye, standing at the door. "Little girl, what is wrong with you?"

Chasity walked into the room picking up Taylor. "Auntie Chasity, I want daddy,"

"Didn't mommy just say she was going to see about you seeing your daddy soon? I think you need to clean out those ears little girl." Chasity started wiggling her fingers in her ear making her laugh. She came in right on time to calm her down.

Taylor laughed harder each time Chasity tickled her ears. "Okay Auntie Chasity, okay."

"Are you done acting mean towards mommy." Taylor shook her head "yes" as Chasity put her back down.

Taylor walked over and kissed me, wiping my face. "Mommy, I'm sorry, I'm not going to be mean anymore."

"Come here sweetie, it's okay. Mommy understands. I know you miss him."

"Chasity, what happened to the side of your arm?" I said distracted by the large bruise that covered her left arm.

"Clumsy me, I was rushing, trying to get out of the house to go to work the other day and hit the wall," she said rubbing on her bruise.

"Okay, well you need to start watching where you are going and slow down. Oh, Seth left, but he told Grandma he would be here around eight o'clock to pick you up. I thought I would tell you, because I doubt Grandmother was going to."

"Okay thanks BB, I better get ready. Seth is going to be here before you know it."

Chasity was the only one that called me BB. I liked it better then Butterball. "Chasity, how did you meet Seth?"

"I met him one night when I went to the club with Dominque. Why you ask?"

"I'm just curious. Does he make you happy?"

"Yes, he does – very."

"He seems different from the other guys you dated," I said trying my best not to sound like he was the worst she has ever been with.

"You mean guys like Daniel, huh? It is time for the family to let that relationship go."

"Well, we all liked Daniel a lot."

"Carmen, that's over, I have moved on, but yes, Seth makes me happy and we are in love."

I couldn't help but wonder how if Seth made Chasity so happy, how come she constantly looked down onto the floor when she talked about him.

"Well, that's good to hear," I said grabbing the twin's hands as we exited the room. "Oh yeah, Chasity, I'm going to have the girls a birthday party at the house in two weeks, do you think you can help me with it?"

"Sure, let me talk to Seth to see what he has planned," she said like she needed his approval. She quickly changed when she saw the look on my face. "I mean, I'm going to see if Seth can bring his kids, as long as it's not any drama with his babies' mothers. That's the reason why he doesn't see his kids as much, because they all want to be with him."

'Oh really,' I thought to myself.

"He is a really great man. One of Seth's daughter's mothers told me, so many lies, saying he treated her like this and like that when they were together. She is so jealous of our relationship, but I had to let her know that regardless of the lies she told, I wasn't going anywhere."

Talking to Chasity was like Déjà vu`. For some reason when I talked to her, it was like I was Aunt Isabel and she was me a few months ago trying to convince me they had the perfect relationship. The only thing I could do was pray that she hadn't gotten herself involved with Mr. Wrong. But for now, I had to get home and prepare to do it all over again tomorrow.

The next day I couldn't stop thinking about Chastity as I prepared for work, but when I got there I thought, *'Here we go again.'* I hated working 2nd shift. The time punished me as it ticked slowly. "Welcome to Mega Burgers & Fries, how may I help you?"

"Let me get a large strawberry shake and a small order of fries,"

'She sounds like somebody I know,' I thought as I took her order. "Okay, that will be $6.09. Please drive around to the next window."

A white, Range Rover with twenty-four-inch chrome rims pulled up to the drive thru window. I lifted my head from making the shake when I heard, "Carmen?"

"Natalie, is that you?"

Natalie Lopez was my friend from middle school. She also lived in Smithstone James apartments when we were younger. I hadn't seen her in years. We were friends on multiple social network sites, but I didn't know she was rolling like this. "Girl, I thought you were in Texas and married from what I heard? I asked your sister about you and she said that you hadn't lived in Florida for over two years."

"How embarrassing?' I thought.

"Well, there was a change of plans. My twins and I moved back to Florida about seven months now."

"Oh okay, that's cool, so where are you living?"

I did not want to broadcast the fact that I was back in the hood, but what other choice did I have. "I'm staying in Smithstone James Apartments. They have really upgraded," making sure she knew they weren't the same as when we were younger.

"Yeah, they did that about two years ago. I moved from over there about a year ago. Things had gotten pretty hard for me. I have a son and daughter, and their father was incarcerated at the time. I thank God, it's not how it was before, you know. He has really been blessing us."

I didn't know how to come out and ask her where she worked, so I could apply tomorrow. I was so anxious in knowing what she did for a living. If she was living in the projects just a year ago and now driving a Range Rover, I had to know what she was doing. I guess the stunned expression on my face told her what I was thinking, because the next thing she said was like a million dollars.

"I see... nice car!"

"Thank you. But this car is extra. I mean it may be nice, but nothing beats anything more than living your life according to God's plan."

"You know Carmen; anyone's situation can change if they have faith, believe it and put in the work."

I so badly wanted to tell her how I was waiting on my situation to change. "Sorry Carmen, I'm acting like there are not a hundred cars behind me waiting on their food. Here is a ten, and my business card, keep the change."

I stared at the card thinking, *'Wow, she's an entrepreneur.'*

"I own a boutique about three blocks from here. Give me a call, you should come by and visit."

"Yeah, sure, I definitely will."

"Okay Chica, talk to you later." I couldn't take my eyes off her car as she pulled off. What she said made something inside of me jump. I stood for a moment thinking about my destiny and purpose. All of a sudden, the faith I did have immediately went to another level. I stood believing I was greater than working at a burger joint, still struggling to pay my bills, stressed and depressed.

After seeing Natalie, I started believing there was more to my life than this. Lost in my thoughts I forgot I was supposed to be taking orders. "Hello! Is anyone there?"

Lloyd walked over to me with an attitude, "Carmen, take the orders girl! Get out of la-la land!"

"I'm so sorry. Welcome to Mega Burgers & Fries, can I take your order?" I said rolling my eyes.

Later that night as we closed Lloyd acted like something was on his mind. "Hey Lloyd, I'm having the girls a 5th birthday party, do you think you can bring your nephew?" He acted as though he was in a daze. "Lloyd, you okay?"

"Oh, I'm good."

"Lloyd, you've been acting very weird lately. What's going on with you?"

"Girl nothing, let's finish cleaning up so we can get out of here."

"Lloyd, I know you, and I pray whatever it is God gets you through it. Everything is going to be alright," I said, putting my hand on his shoulder.

Lloyd looked at me, laughed then said. "Girl, God is taking care of everything, I promise you that!"

"That's great, but you seem different. What's up? Talk to me?"

"Okay Carmen, I haven't told too many people because I wanted to make sure everything was a done deal first. My mentor said to wait, but I'll share with my best friend.

"A mentor – is this my friend Lloyd I'm talking to?"

"Yes girl, it's me," he said laughing. "Carmen, I may not have ever told you this, but you have inspired me for years. You've always believed in me, and encouraged me even when I didn't believe in myself."

"Wow, I did? I had no idea." Him saying that made me feel peace on the inside. It gave me joy – it made me feel very happy.

"Do you remember that day I talked to you about a year ago when you were still living in Texas."

"I guess Lloyd, please get to the point."

"Well, you said I had to believe that everything was going to be alright. You told me about the church you were attending and that Pastor Brian guy. After I talked to you I started going to my mother's church until I could watch

Pastor Brian online. You know at the time I couldn't afford the internet."

"You started watching Pastor Brian?"

"Yes! And I can't thank you enough for telling me about him. Why didn't you tell me he was an ex-gang banger and drug dealer?"

"For real, Lloyd? Wow! I had no idea that was his story. I remember Aunt Isabel said that he had a powerful testimony, but I had already left Texas when he shared it during one of his sermons."

"Carmen, this is between me and you, don't you dare tell anyone,"

"Okay Lloyd, I wouldn't tell anyone. Now please, get to the point."

"Carmen, his testimony almost had me in tears. Then he said something that gave me a little hope. I didn't even know what faith was. I heard people talk about it, but didn't really understand it. I didn't know it was something you hoped for in your life. Pastor said if God turned his life around, then He could turn anyone's life around. Carmen, I can't tell you what that did for me."

"Lloyd that is great!" I was getting very excited hearing my friend speak the way he was. I had never heard him speak in such a way before. He was so different – so positive.

"When I met my mentor, Tamela's father, he told me how much potential he saw in me."

"Speaking of Tamela, when am I going to meet her?" I asked in a sarcastic voice.

"You will meet her soon, now back to my story," he said with a serious look. "Her dad told me that I had potential," he said pointing his self in the chest. "Carmen, my mom told me all my life that I would be nothing. I would always be like my father, a dead beat, drug dealer and drug addict. I only thought I'd be what I was told all my life. I didn't know I could be anything else,"

"Lloyd, Jesus said "nothing is impossible to those who believe." And you are not what your mother has spoken over your life."

It was funny how as I told him those words, I thought about my own situation pertaining to my father. It was like I was speaking to myself as I encouraged Lloyd. I was not what Pretty Boy said I was.

"I know I'm not! I don't receive any of that no more. I have turned my life around completely. I got saved about four months ago and have been attending church with Tamela and her family."

"Oh really!?"

For a moment I felt like I had no idea who this guy was I was talking to. "We attend St. Peterson Ministries on East Concord Street. Hey, you want to come Sunday?"

"I haven't been at church in a while. Yes, that would be cool."

Wow, a few months ago I acted as if I were ashamed to tell him I was saved, seeking God and going to church. Now here he was openly telling me about his salvation. "Okay, but this is what I was really trying to tell you."

"Lloyd that's what I've been waiting to hear!"

"So, you know I can sing and rap, but stopped years ago because my mom would always tell me I sounded horrible and should only sing in the shower. Well, Mr. Morris, my mentor heard me singing one day and one of his friends is a big-time producer who has produced several popular artists."

"Really?"

"Well, I have been in the studio recording some of my songs and my first single goes worldwide in a few weeks!"

I was shocked and couldn't believe all this time my friend had been busy because he'd been in the studio. He could have told me. "And guess what?" his face lit up like kids on Christmas Day.

"What? What? Just tell me Lloyd, I don't want to guess," I was too excited.

"If all goes well, I'll be signing a $300,000 contract as an artist with one of the most popular record companies, The Brownstone Brothers."

"Oh my gosh! Are you serious?! Lloyd, I can't believe it. I'm so happy for you!"

"Carmen, there was something I heard Pastor Brian, say – he said everything we need and who we are, is already inside of us."

"What do you mean Lloyd?"

"Carmen, we all have gifts from God. Like singing and rapping are my gifts. Who knows, I may even have more than those two. I'm surely going to be asking God," he said laughing. "You have gifts as well; you have to find out what they are."

"Lloyd, truth is, I have battled for years not knowing who I am, and if I don't know who I am, how can I find out what my gifts are? I heard Pastor Brian say that before to, but I don't know where to start."

"Carmen, who knows all of the instructions and functions of a product?"

"The person who made it, right? Lloyd is that a trick question?"

"Right Carmen, the manufacturer! Well, God is our creator, so we must ask Him to reveal to us who we are. It's the process, I had to do it, you have to do it, we all have to do it. I told God I surrender to the plan that He designed for my life, that is the key. And He started to guide me according to HIS will and not my own, and it went from there."

"Carmen, one Scripture I meditate on daily is Jeremiah 29:11. If you meditate on that, you will know God has a plan and purpose for your life. It says plain and clear that the plans that God has for our life is for us to prosper, not to bring disaster, but to give us a hope for the future"

"Okay Lloyd, I will read it."

"Make sure you do, I did, and let Him guide you."

Lloyd had laid some heavy stuff on me. This whole day had been a wake-up call for my life. Hearing Natalie's testimony, and hearing Lloyd's news had me thinking about Pastor Brian's message about, "Dreams turning into a reality."

I started to think if it could happen for Natalie and Lloyd then it could happen for me. I couldn't wait to get home tonight to start praying, reading the Bible and talking to God so that He could show me who I am. I am somebody! I was created for a purpose! I now refused to believe that purpose doesn't live inside of me.

Overcoming The Battle

Chapter Sixteen

After the girl's birthday party Aunt Isabel took them back to Texas with her for the rest of the summer. By the time they return it will be time for them to start kindergarten. I missed them so much, but I understood they have to see the other side of their family, and I also needed the break.

When I spoke to Mackenzie, she was so excited about her new baby brother. She said she was glad to be a big sister and loved him so much. Devin was proudly showing off his son. I felt myself get a little irritated and hurt hearing the girls talk about their father's new baby.

I wanted to ask him who he thought he was, having his baby all up in our daughter's face, but quickly came to myself. It was time for me to move on. I had to do some more praying and talking to God, because I didn't want bad thoughts or feelings towards Devin to affect my girls.

I hoped no else would have to experience the Devin Diaz, I experienced. Anyways, I didn't have time to worry about Devin and his life; I needed to focus on finding out *"Who Carmen is and my purpose in life?"* I have lived a façade long enough.

Devin agreed to send six hundred dollars a month once the girls returned home. For a second I thought he was taking the cheap way out. I could've sent him to court to pursue more, but I will see if he holds up his end of the bargain.

When Aunt Isabel came to pick up the girls she bought me a book titled, *"What Was I Purposed For?"* It was a forty-five-day focus on discovering your purpose in life. The instructions were to read a chapter or two a day and focus on the matter being learned.

It was a very powerful book which cross referenced Scriptures that spoke about God having plans for our life. It also had the Scripture at the beginning of each chapter Lloyd suggested I read daily, Jeremiah 29:11. The more I meditated on Jeremiah 29:11 which says, ***"For I know the plans I have for you, declares the Lord, plans* to prosper *you and not to harm you, plans to give you hope and a future."***

The more I believed it and knew how much God loves me and created me for purpose. My daily goal was to strive to develop a better version of me and a closer relationship with God to discover my purpose. I had been attending St. Peterson Ministries for the past month and enjoyed the powerful messages. They had two services, which I could fit it into my work schedule.

I tried to attend the mid-week services, but most of the time I was unable to. There was no getting around it; I had no choice since I had become the shift manager. The shift manager position was a plus, with a dollar increase, but the negative side was all the extra hours I had to work. I wasn't going to complain, it was progress.

Chapter Seventeen

Tamela, Lloyd's girlfriend was beautiful. She looked like someone out of a magazine. She sang background on Lloyd's album, while he was trying to convince her to do her own album. I could tell she made him happy – they make each other happy.

Lloyd had said last week he was ready to start ring shopping and wanted to pop the question. I laughed at the fact that we had grown up and were adults, and now Lloyd was ready to settle down and get married. I couldn't have been happier for the two of them.

It had been thirty days since Lloyd's first single, *"Loving You with All of Me,"* went worldwide. It received ten times more results than he needed to sign his contract with The Brownstone Brothers Record Company. Lloyd said Mr. Morris was now his manager and would be traveling with him, and they were leaving in ten days to start his tour to promote his album. The single was hitting the top of the charts on so many radio stations around the country.

I praised God for what He was doing in Lloyd's life. It built my faith, believing He would do wonders in my life as well. I now had a mentor who was helping me along the way; Victoria Singleton, founder of Singleton's ministries.

A few months after moving back to Florida I met Victoria at Darby's, a store not far from my house. She was a complete stranger who walked up to me and told me how God had plans for my life. She really encouraged me although at first, I thought it was a little weird. When she pinpointed things in my life and encouraged me in such a way, it was a sign she was God sent. Who would have ever thought a stranger handing me a card would be such an impact in my life.

I knew greater was coming from the conversations Victoria and I had. I remember days before meeting her Pastor Susan Bridges message and Victoria spoke the same words of encouragement to me; another sign she was God sent. I felt like God was trying to show me there was more for my life with the way I met her. We went to lunch together, the movies, we shopped together, I even started attending her weekly Women's Empowerment Group.

Victoria suggested I start receiving counseling to completely heal from past encounters. At first, I wasn't sure about it, but after she told me how her experience helped her heal, I decided to give it a try. She referred me to Dr. Celena Barnoff. I knew it was helping me when my dreams and thoughts weren't as bad as before.

Dr. Barnoff counseling sessions incorporated the Word of God and I always tried to remember what she said. She told me if any thoughts or something occurs to steal, kill, or destroy my joy, peace, or etc. it was not of God. Victoria asked me to share my story at her women's empowerment meeting in two weeks, but I didn't know if I was ready.

I noticed my phone ringing, and Pretty Boy's number was flashing across the Caller ID. I had been anxious to speak to him, because I didn't know what was going on. He didn't even attend the twin's birthday party, but Nancy was there with a lot of gifts for the girls. I think she bought so many, hoping it would cover up the fact that my dad wasn't at the party.

"Hello."

"Hey, Butterball."

"Pretty Boy, I've been calling you for months, where have you been?"

"I know Carmen; I know; you are not going to believe what has been going on. Please, brace yourself for what I'm about to tell you."

"What is going on? You missed the girl's birthday party."

"Carmen, I promise to make it up to you. I had to find work in Tennessee."

"Why are you in Tennessee?"

"To help your Uncle Greg, you're not going to believe this. Your Uncle Greg is being accused of having sex with a fourteen-year-old. The accusations caused him to lose his job, not to mention his wife is ready to leave him."

"The little girl lives across the street and is making up these false accusations. Greg was telling me how everyone says she's fast. I've been here trying to help with his attorney fees and bills. I don't know how much longer your Aunt Marisa is going to stick around. This is a very hard time for them."

I could only imagine what his wife was going through. She was a sweet and caring lady and didn't deserve any of this. Pretty Boy said she had been prescribed pills for depression and that she didn't know what to believe. One moment she believed her husband was innocent, and the next moment she felt like he may have done it. This was not the first rumor she had heard about her husband.

I listened as my father continued to defend his friend. "They had no evidence or anything for months. It has all been based off what the little girl said, but this morning they found some belongings buried in Greg's backyard. They said they don't believe they are hers, but they still have to check, and get the results from the DNA."

"They think it maybe something that could help or not help with the case. I can't wait until they run it for DNA results to show all of this was a lie. Then they can throw the case out. I know she's a child, but she is going to pay for the trouble she has caused."

I had gone into a daze and no longer could hear anything Pretty Boy said. He was so confident it was all a lie. So many thoughts ran through my head, from the visits to the park, the water park, the beach, movies, you name it, and Uncle Greg took me there. But after every adventure he would take his hand and rub all over my body. Kissing me, telling me not to tell anyone; that it was our secret and he wanted to make me feel good.

I was ten years old the first time he inserted his penis into my virgin vagina. He didn't go all the way because it was too painful. Actually, it was excruciating. I didn't know it was wrong at the time. Then there were times when I think I actually enjoyed it, it was kind of twisted.

For years it bothered me, but sex was all I wanted. After my experience with him I used to sneak and watch pornography. Sex, sex, and more sex always ran through my mind. I've learned through counseling that the molestation and rape were the reason for the uncontrollable sexual desires.

Pretty Boy sounded so sad; so, hurt for what his perverted friend was going through. I couldn't take it anymore. "Pretty Boy this is my fault! "I should have said something when he was doing it to me. It was the longest three years ever," I cried.

"Baby, I know you're upset to think someone would do this to your Uncle Greg, but this is not your fault."

It was like he didn't hear anything I said. "Daddy, I need you to listen to what I'm trying to say."

"Okay baby, I'm listening," he said caught off guard that I called him Daddy.

"Daddy, it's true, I believe he did it. No wait, I know he did it! He molested and raped me from the ages of seven to ten!"

It was only the third time I had told anyone what had happened to me. I had held it in for twenty years – twenty years too long. I told Pretty Boy about all the adventures and how he molested and raped me after them. Apparently, that was payment for the gifts and trips I received.

"But Butterball, if that's true why didn't you say something when it happened? I mean, I thought you would have mentioned it to me or your mother."

The fact he said, *"if it were true,"* took me completely out of my calling him "daddy" mode. I couldn't believe he acted as if he didn't know whether to believe me

165

or not. When I needed him more than anything to step up and take the "daddy" role, it felt like he was turning his back on me more than ever. "What do you mean, if it's true?! It is true, and that ole child molester deserves everything he got coming to him. Pretty Boy, do you seriously not believe me?!"

"I didn't mean to say that Butterball. I guess I'm just surprised. I couldn't imagine Greg hurting anyone."

"That's it Pretty Boy, it doesn't matter what you couldn't have imagined. You trusted a man that was smiling all in your face and screwing your daughter when she was ten years old! You have no idea the torment I've experienced these years. I felt ashamed, like I did something wrong. I didn't even know how to love myself. You were never the father you should have been!"

"Butterball, I'm sorry you had to go through that. I'm sorry; I know I wasn't the father I should have been. That's the past, what more do you want from me? I can't change it!"

"You may not be able to change the past, but you are not trying to change now! I just told you what Uncle Greg did, and you can't even be here for me. Well Great! I've been so brainwashed I continued to call him Uncle. Maybe it's because you've never been there, but you could at least try."

"Look, I see where this is going, but these past few months have been hell. I don't have time for this. I will talk to you when we can have a better conversation, my phone is going dead. I will call you tomorrow once the DNA results are in."

"That's okay Pretty Boy, I'm used to you running from situations and not handling them. Do me a favor and don't call me. You can take yourself, Greg, and those DNA results and go straight to hell!" I hung up the phone crying even harder. It was meant for this day to come, and if Pretty Boy didn't believe me now, he would one day.

Pretty Boy had called back three times, leaving a message each time. I felt disgusted, and started to doubt the invitation from Victoria to share my story at her Women's Empowerment Meeting. I had to pray and talk to God about this. I wanted to share my story to help others, but now I was second guessing moving forward.

Overcoming The Battle

Sex No More

She always talked about wanting a God-fearing man,
But as soon as she felt a touch from a hand,
Down came those pants.
She was talked about so badly,
Always called a whore,
But they never knew that deep down inside,
All she wanted was more.
She adored him, daddy's best-friend,
She trusted him with her life.
She didn't know that in her heart one day,
It would feel like she was stabbed with a knife.
See, what they didn't know was the seed that was sown,
When she was seven and he was three times eleven,
Rubbing all over her body,
Telling her it's our special secret,
So please don't tell nobody,
So, all throughout life she had desires of sex,
After getting up from one man,
All she could think about was the next.
Until that day came, and she said,
I give up, I can't do this anymore.
Lord it's You that I want to adore.
She fought with the battle inside of her for years,
Held back thousands and thousands of tears.
So, to God she gave herself away,
Realizing that now when she met a man,

They didn't always have to get in the bed and play.
God took her and made a successful business woman.
Now today, she travels around the world
To minister and inspire
To help save other broken little girls.
God built her up to trust again,
He was preparing her to be ready for
When He sent her a God-fearing man,
They became husband and wife,
She loved him and he loved her with his life.

Chapter Eighteen

The DNA test results came in the next day just like Pretty Boy said. The little girl's belongings buried in Greg's back yard did in fact contain her and Uncle Greg's DNA. Pretty Boy sent me a text message since I wasn't answering his calls.

Grandma had called Aunt Marisa to check on her, and she told her how they had become acquainted with the little girl across the street. She and Uncle Greg would take turns watching after her when she got out of school until her parents got off from work. Aunt Marisa had no idea it had been going on since the little girl was ten.

I prayed for her and any other little girls he may have sexually violated. What makes people do things like that to kids? I know during my counseling sessions, Dr. Barnoff said most of the time the violator has been violated themselves. She said most people never share it with anyone and some end up hurting others. I was sickened at the thought.

Pretty Boy had been calling me for five weeks straight, but I wasn't ready to speak to him. He had to have left me over a hundred messages apologizing. On one of the messages he was crying. He said he blamed himself because he didn't protect his little girl like he should have. He said he should've been more aware of what was going on, and didn't know if he could forgive himself.

Truth is I don't know if Pretty Boy would have been aware of what was going on unless he stopped all the partying and drugging he was doing. I mean, for heaven's sake, this was a guy he had been best friends with since the ninth grade. He considered him family, someone he thought he could trust, but it didn't matter if he was a friend of the family, it was still wrong.

I had heard and read so many testimonies from women who were sexually violated by their father, brothers, and cousins – all different kinds of family members. It really made me angry knowing that so many women's innocence had been stolen from them at very young ages. Even Victoria had been raped by her own father and uncle when she was younger. It made me so angry; I wanted to do something to bring awareness to put a stop to it.

When I told my testimony at the Women's Empowerment session, there was a crowd of forty women in the room. I didn't know that many women would be there. I had to admit I was very nervous at first, but had been praying to God for days, letting Him know He had to help me when I gave my story. After I finished speaking there was an open discussion where some of the women told their stories for the first time.

It made me feel better after telling my story. I was glad I could be a blessing to others, so they could open up and start releasing what they had been holding inside. I had to admit, the first time I shared my story was a success. My voice wasn't as shaky as I thought it was going to be, which was surprising, because it was very shaky when I practiced.

It's like I decided to be a willing vessel and God had His way in helping me share my story.

I had heard before that you never know who could be in a room with you or who you are entertaining. I came to find that Victoria was good friends with a lady name Alexis Townsend, who was a DJ at a radio station in Orlando. She was at the meeting and asked me to share my story in a radio interview. Alexis said my story was very inspiring and she believed I could encourage others and impact more lives telling it on the radio. I couldn't imagine going public with my story, but it was an experience I will never forget.

During the radio interview Alexis asked several questions about my story and I only hoped my response would encourage other women to use their voice.

"Carmen how has this impacted you to keep what happened bottled up inside after these years."

"Well I felt worthless, like nothing, I felt dirty and ashamed, like I had done something wrong, and it was my fault. I believe therefore many women are afraid to open up about been violated."

After I made that statement, so many women started calling into the radio station. They said they felt the same way, having turned to food, sex, or drugs to fill that empty feeling inside.

Although we may use these as a means of filling the void, it was doing more self-destruction. I shared how only God could heal and fill the voids, we try to use other things to, but those things are only temporary. His fulfillment was permanent while ours was temporary. I couldn't help the tears that welled up in my eyes while listening to some of their stories. After I opened up to Victoria that night on the call, I started rebuilding my relationship with God. He opened his arms right back up to me like I never fell off. I was glad to have someone like Victoria and Natalie to be a part of my life.

Natalie came to the empowering meeting to support me while I was speaking. She and I started hanging out about a week after I saw her at Mega Burgers & Fries. She was so empowering and encouraging. She always said even though Smithstone James had been remodeled, it hadn't changed.

It really bothered her how people who lived there settled, but could have more if only they believed more was available. "Carmen, you know my mindset was broken at one point of time, but it's possible for anyone's mindset to change. There is always hope and a possibility for your mindset to change when you step out of your comfort zone. Think and start looking at things differently."

"You know I didn't believe that before, but I do now."

I want to do something to impact lives to let people know it's possible. I mean, look at us. We grew up in the projects and I'm not forgetting where I came from, but God has more available for us."

"I agree. So, what do you plan on doing, Natalie?"

"I plan on getting my voice heard. Maybe start some meetings or something. The subsidized housing was only to give us a push, a little help. But sometimes it becomes a family agenda, generation of families living there and never moving, and I believe it's because they believe there is nothing more available or they don't deserve anything more."

"So, have you tried to talk to someone at the office at Smithstone James apartments?"

"Carmen, I have been able to get into other places, but they won't budge. I presented the whole layout in educating people who live there on their finances, how to budget, credit, and how to get themselves in a better position where they can buy a house."

"So, you keep trying until it happens."

"That is exactly what I'm going to do. Smithstone was meant to be temporary, not a crutch. It almost makes me feel like the people in the office don't want us to do better."

"Do you know there's a lady who has lived in those apartments for fifteen years? Her daughters grew up there, and moved back with their kids. I just want to see people do better Carmen. They deserve better."

"I know you do. Hey, look I will be praying for you, pray that you have the faith knowing God is going to get you through those doors."

"You're right. And I will do the same. I believe it's part of God's purpose for me to get through those doors. But I won't let this be a distraction or stop me from an agenda to help others."

"That's the spirit!"

After praying, fasting, and believing, God opened those doors for Natalie. Three weeks later, she was approved to hold her meetings at Smithstone James apartments.

Sometimes delayed does not mean denied. I was very excited for her, and I knew she was going to do a great job!

Chapter Nineteen

Grandma Ruth Anne was having her sixty-sixth birthday party, but I couldn't attend since I had to work. When I pulled up at her house she was dressed in her red blouse and black skirt that fit her curvy hips. There was no doubt where my sisters and I had inherited those curves.

My grandmother had been waiting at the door and immediately walked out when she saw me. I had only made it half way to the driveway before she was at my passenger door. "Give me a second lady – let me unlock the door, please. You know I could have come in and at least escorted you to the car, right?" I said, as she sat down in the passenger seat.

"Carmen, I was ready to get out of that house. I was dressed hours ago. Your uncle and cousins are about to drive me crazy."

When she gave me a kiss on the cheek her perfume smelled so good. It was the same familiar perfume she wore when I was a little girl. "They can't be that bad." I couldn't help but laugh at the face she was making as she spoke.

"Well, I need you to know they are that bad," she said rolling her eyes. Then she leaned over and kissed me again, and hugged me tight before I pulled out of the driveway.

"Baby, I'm so sorry for what you experienced, I had no idea. Your daddy told me about what Greg did to you. If I had known, I would have killed him dead."

I looked at her like, "*What did you say?*"

"Grandma, you have always told us that vengeance is the Lord's. It's okay, I have decided to forgive him, and I know everything is going to be alright. He has some long thinking to do for at least thirty to fifty years in jail, unless they give him the death penalty."

I shared my story with her as we drove to her favorite restaurant and told her I felt better each time I told it. I also explained how I wanted to help others by sharing my story. "Carmen, I am proud of you baby, you let God use you. As I watched you grow up, you have always been encouraging to others and lifting their spirits. Baby, I could only imagine how you felt keeping that in all these years."

"I'm going to be okay, I am okay, and I promise you it only made me stronger," I said kissing her on the cheek.

We pulled up at the restaurant and she handed me a letter she had received earlier that day addressed to me. The address on the stamp was from a nursing home in East Tampa. I opened the letter and it was from my Grandma Stella. "It's from Mrs. Stella!" I shouted as I opened up the envelope.

"I thought she would have fallen over dead now, with a heart as evil and bitter as hers. What does she want?"

"Don't be like that grandma, now you know that's not nice. No need holding grudges."

"I'm not holding grudges Carmen, but I didn't like how that lady did you and your sisters. You couldn't call her grandmother. She acted like she hated y'all. It hurt me to see the look in you and your sister's eyes when you asked your mother how come y'all don't see your grandmother any longer."

"Every time, your mother never had an answer. I guess I'm just wondering what she wants now after all these years," she said with her nostrils flared.

"Grandma Stella said she is in a nursing home after having two strokes. She also suffers from high blood pressure and diabetes. She has been in a nursing home for the past five months and she says she wants to see me."

"Are you going to go see her baby? Carmen, I don't know if that's a good idea."

"I believe I am. She's reaching out now; I owe it to myself to hear her out."

Several times I had reached out to her, but never received a response. Now, finally she decided to respond to the letter I sent her almost a year ago. I was excited, overwhelmed, and shocked all at the same time. I couldn't wait to tell Chasity and Charlotte and wondered if they would be excited as well.

"Come on Foxy Lady, we're here. Let's go celebrate."

Overcoming The Battle

Chapter Twenty

It had been six months since Lloyd's single was released and the outcome was amazing. Tonight Lloyd's manager, Mr. Morris, Tamela's father had thrown Lloyd a dinner for the success of his record. It was an amazing night.

My feet were hurting from the heels I had worn, and I couldn't wait until they were off my feet. I took them off immediately getting into my car, placing my bare feet onto the floor mat. Lloyd's dinner was very nice and Mr. Morris, his soon to be father-in-law, had the most gorgeous and biggest home I had ever laid eyes on.

The dinner was a surprise for Lloyd, he thought it was a dinner with only immediate family and close friends for his birthday which was in a week. It was actually a dinner to recognize him for a job well done on his record. But the tables turned when he surprised Tamela by proposing to her. Tamela and Lloyd made a great couple, and the glow on her face when he proposed was priceless. Lloyd introduced me to Tamela's cousin Thomas who had been giving me the eye all night. If he wasn't as cute as he was, I would have thought he was a weirdo.

After he introduced us, we talked for about an hour and a half after the dinner was over. When he asked for my number I hesitated for a moment, thinking maybe it wasn't a good idea. I wasn't sure if I was ready to start talking to guys yet, Jesus was my only focus and that's all I wanted for now. However, I decided to give him my number – I guessed it wouldn't hurt. Besides, if it did I would change my number in a heartbeat.

When I got in the car I noticed that I had five missed calls and three voice mail messages. My ringer was off, and I hadn't noticed that I had received any calls. Pretty Boy and Grandma had been ringing my phone off the hook. The voicemail my grandmother left was very unnerving.

"Carmen, please hurry! Meet me at the hospital, it's Chasity! Something has happened!"

It was 1:45 in the morning when I arrived at the hospital, and I didn't know what to expect when I got there. I didn't know what was going on that night, but it was crowded. As I walked toward the front desk I could feel the butterflies in my stomach. "Can you please tell me what room Chasity Wilson is in?".

"Yes, down the hall in room 1612, but you can't go back unless your family," she said with an attitude.

"She is my sister," I said trying not to return the attitude.

When I entered the room I noticed Dominque, Chasity's best friend standing at the foot of her bed. Then I saw Grandma sitting in a chair beside Chasity, holding her hand. However, there was one person that I was curious to know where they were. Where was Mr. Seth? He should have been the first person I saw when I walked into the room.

Chasity looked like she had been in an accident. Her left arm was in a sling, she had a busted lip and a bruise above her right eye. "Oh my gosh, are you okay?! What happened?!" I asked running to her side.

Grandma, Chasity and Dominique all stared at me for a moment before anything was said. "I'm okay; I was in a minor car accident."

Chasity looked away as she spoke, and the sound of her voice was shaky. Dominique stared at Chasity with the angriest look on her face. "Car accident Chasity? Really? Are you serious?!"

Chasity gave her a look that said, "Please, shut up."

"Tell the truth before I do. I'm tired of you covering this mess up!"

"Covering what up?"

"Nothing Grandma," Chasity said.

"Oh, it's a big nothing," Dominique said staring at Chasity.

"What is she talking about baby?" Grandma asked.

"Yes, what is she talking about?" I asked.

"Nothing Grandma, it's nothing Carmen," Chasity said taking a deep breath.

"I can't believe you!"

"Dominique, you can leave if you're going to start drama," Chasity said rolling her eyes.

"Drama? You know who the drama maker is. I will leave, but only after your family knows what's been going on with you. Chastity, you have been my best friend for years and I love you too much to see this to continue."

From the words Chasity and Dominique were exchanging, I had no idea what was going on. "Dominique, leave now!"

Dominique looked at Grandma and me as she started to speak. "That no good Seth has been beating on her and kicking her tail like a rag doll, and all she wants to do is cover up for him. What has he done to you Chasity? You never let a man treat you like this before? And every time it happens you blame yourself, saying that it was your fault!"

Chasity never allowed a man to cheat, beat or disrespect her. I noticed since I had moved back home she didn't smile as much. Chasity was always the one that looked down at women who boyfriends abused them. She would always say, "I would never go through that. I wouldn't ever let a man do this or that."

It's funny how at times we can quickly judge someone's else situation, say what we wouldn't do or allow to happen, but no one knows until they are in that situation themselves. Grandma always told us, *"Never say never."*

"I knew that old snake wasn't any good!" Grandma shouted. Here is my phone, you are going to call 911 and press charges on that no good, son of a ...!"

"Grandma!" I shouted before she could finish the rest. She hadn't talked like that in years.

"Chasity, please be honest when I ask you this." I looked her straight in the eyes hoping to only receive the truth. "Is that how you received that bruise on your arm when you claimed you ran into a wall?"

She dropped her head even lower nodding it back and forth saying, "Yes."

I watched the tears fall from her eyes and onto her hospital gown. "It's like I can't leave him alone. I love him too much!"

Then she slowly lifted her head as she tried to explain. "He may have hit me a few times, but I was the only woman he wanted. Daniel humiliated me by cheating on me with all those women. Not to mention the three sexually transmitted diseases he gave me. At least I know there is no one else but me. I caught Daniel with so many women it drove me crazy."

So, there was the truth about what happened to Daniel. Even her best friend didn't know the story behind their break up. I could tell from the look on her face that she had no idea. "Chasity, you said that as if it's okay that he hit you. Just because he doesn't cheat on you doesn't give him the right to put his hands on you. Baby, that's not love, and you don't have to take a man hitting or cheating on you!" Grandma said squeezing her hand.

"If a man loves you he treats you with the upmost respect – nothing less than a queen. You should be treated like a queen, because women are God's precious gifts. We are His diamonds. A man that loves you doesn't put his hands on you. Your grandfather, God rests his soul, treated me like nothing less than a queen, and I treated him like my king. I wish you girls loved yourself enough to know that's not how you are supposed to be treated, instead of putting all this love into these men and they aren't even your husbands."

Grandma tried to keep her composure as she continued. "I want to know when the Bible changed and said for a woman to submit to her boyfriend or kid's father, or baby daddy is what y'all say – Humph!" Grandma shook her head disgusted. "I don't know why some people don't value or know their self-worth. When you don't put limitations, or set standards on how people should treat you in general, you will always allow them to treat you any old kind of way.

"Whether they are putting their hands on you, cheating on you, or speaking to you in a disrespectful way, it's disrespectful. It's not only you females that are taking the disrespect; it's some of these men too. Some of them think because a woman has a pretty face and a fat fanny that she can use him for his money, cheat on him, and talk to him any kind of way. No one has to accept that. God did not put us on this earth to be walked all over or ran over by another human being."

Grandma had a good point. I waited on Devin hand and foot, and that was before he even proposed. We were only a few months into the relationship when I started treating him like he was my husband. The scenery in the hospital made me think about that day in Texas when I left, and the conversation Charlotte and I had.

"Chasity, I went through this same thing with Devin for years, this is not love. This is lust, and knowing the difference is a must, or we will keep falling for lust. You deserve so much better. You can't go back to him, your worth so much more than this," I said as I wiped her tears from her face.

"But, what if he gets help BB?"

I leaned over and hugged her, "Chasity, I said the same thing about Devin. But what if he doesn't get help and you end up dead first?"

I wanted to stay at the hospital all night, but it was late, and I was afraid of driving home sleepy. "Look, I'm exhausted. I'm going home to get some rest. Chasity, are they keeping you for the night or are they discharging you?"

"No, I'm going home. I'm waiting on the nurse to come back with my release papers."

"Tomorrow morning I'm coming over; I want you to talk with someone. You don't have to say anything; just listen to what they have to say. I love you, good night."

"Okay, I love you too BB, see you later."

"Dominique, you're a great friend. Thank you so much. Chasity don't be mad at her; she's only trying to save your life."

The next day I called Aunt Isabel to check on the girls, and then asked her if she could talk to Chasity. Aunt Isabel sent her before and after pictures of her incident to my cell phone. I prayed Chasity would see Aunt Isabel's pictures and realize she deserved better.

When I arrived at my grandmother's house, I called Aunt Isabel and let her speak to Chasity. My sister wept while Aunt Isabel shared her story. Just like me, she couldn't believe what she was seeing or hearing. I hated seeing my sister go through the same thing I went through.

After leaving the hospital the other night, I was up all night pacing the floor in my apartment. It was only two nights prior to Chasity's incident that my neighbor had called the police on her abusive boyfriend. So many ideas started running through my head about domestic violence, molestation, and the adversity so many women deal with.

There was an idea that I had shared with Natalie, and she kept asking me when I was going to do something with it. Natalie always said that she believed that if anyone has an idea they should never let it go to waste. She would always tease and say, "You don't want anyone else to pick up your idea, do you?"

The following Monday, I called my Aunt Megan, my dad's sister who was an attorney with her own law firm in Jacksonville Florida. I always admired and looked up to her. Growing up, I always hoped to be successful just like her. I shared with my aunt the idea of establishing a business to inspire other women who had battled adversity in life like me, my sister, and others. I wanted to call it, *"Lovely Prosperous Ladies."*

The mission was to empower women to live a life full of prosperity despite the adversity they may have experienced. To empower women to live life to the extent of what it has to offer. This would mean, living healthy lifestyles, being in successful businesses, relationships, jobs, and to live a complete life of purpose, joy and happiness. The way God's original design was for our lives.

Aunt Megan listened as I told her my idea of visiting girls in foster homes, and women shelters where I could share my story. Also, to create an online clothing store where empowerment clothing, such as: shirts, hats, jackets and other items would be sold. I also shared my story with her about Uncle Greg. I told her I was determined to forgive and inspire others, instead of walking around hurt with unforgiveness.

Unforgiveness is for the person holding it inside, they must release it. You will feel so much better once you LET IT GO! Before, I felt as though Uncle Greg had some type of power or control over my life, because I had blocked out the incident and was in denial for years. I didn't realize the unforgiveness I held in my heart until I allowed God to reveal it from seeking Him.

Aunt Megan said she was so sorry about what happened, but that she was proud of me and would do anything to help. She gave me information to different companies where I could write out my business plan; receive business loans, and, even some grants I wouldn't have to pay back. I was so excited and ready to make a difference in the world.

God was giving me my beauty for my ashes. I didn't understand it God spoke it to me the night I called Victoria. Now I understood what it means when it's said, "What the enemy meant for bad, God was turning it around and was going to receive all the glory for it."

Overcoming The Battle

Chapter Twenty-One

Thinking about what my sister and I had gone through made me think about my mother. For years I watched her try to have a relationship with her mother, my grandmother, Mrs. Stella. Maybe visiting her would give the closure my mother never received. I wasn't sure if going to visit her would give closure, but I thought it was worth a try.

I had started visiting Mrs. Stella at the nursing home and it was during one of my visits that she had told me her story. As she told her story, I couldn't help but notice how this seventy-two-year-old woman looked as if she was in her nineties, even close to one hundred years old. She must have had a rough life. She said she had been hurting for years and it saddened her that she didn't get to make things right before my mother died.

Mrs. Stella said I could call her Grandma or Mimi, but it felt kind of weird I must admit. She said after being in the nursing home for two months she became friends with a lady name Peggy Sue Hicks. Her son was married to a black woman. She said she watched the way her friend Peggy Sue loved on her daughter-in-law and biracial grandchildren, and she didn't understand it.

Mrs. Stella stopped dealing with my mother when she found out she had secretly married my father and got pregnant with me. I interrupted in the middle of her story, not meaning to, but I couldn't help it. "Why couldn't you be like your friend Peggy Sue?"

"Carmen, it was difficult finding out my daughter was carrying a half black child."

A thrust of anger rose up within me for a moment and tears started to stream down my face. I could feel my mother's pain from all those years. "You had twenty-four years to get it right, but you let her die without doing so. Your own daughter, I just don't understand!"

"You are right. Everything you are saying is absolutely right! And there is no excuse, but the way I was raised mixing blacks with whites was an abomination. Carmen, I only believed in what I knew all my life."

"You would barley even look at us! When we were younger we couldn't even call you Grandma. You, treated us like animals. All the letters I've sent you for years and now you're reaching out?"

"Baby, I'm sorry!" Her voice began to shake as she started to cry. "I wish I could change the hands of time. I was so stupid and ignorant. I wish my daughter was still here. She was my only child. And I let something so evil and stupid make me treat her like she wasn't even my child. The pain I feel on a day to day basis is something I wouldn't wish on my worst enemy. Carmen, I didn't get it right with my daughter, but I hope to get it right with her daughters will count for something."

Although she was wrong, I reached over to hug and console her. I could tell her heart was different. "Mrs. Stella as hard as it is, knowing how you did my mother and her children, I forgive you. And I know God has forgiven you. But you must also forgive yourself."

Growing up my mom told us her mother said she wasn't prejudice, she just didn't think races should mix. But contrary to my grandmother's beliefs my mother never saw color. At an early age I was taught that people were not born with racism or hate in their heart, that behavior is taught to others. Our mother raised us differently from how she was raised. She told us her grandparents raised her mother that way, and that's how she tried to raise her, but my mother wasn't having it.

"I apologize for interrupting, but you were saying?"

"It's okay. It's because of Peggy Sue, that I see different now. God brought her into my life for this specific reason. But I asked her one day. Peggy Sue, can I ask you a question?"

"What is it Stella?"

"I'm curious as to how it makes you feel knowing your son is married to a colored girl?"

"Excuse me?!!!" she asked with her eyes stretched wide-eyed.

"I have you to know that I love LaShanda as if she was my own daughter. She loves my son, he loves her, and they make one another happy! What are you talking about with all this foolishness? Colored? What year are you living in? You know the terms used today are either African-American or black, right?!!"

"I know Peggy, but I'm used to saying colored, because that is what momma and daddy used to say all the time."

"Stella, I'm going to pray for you."

"Why, I was always told that mixing races was wrong, and that we could possibly even get a disease if we did it."

"So, you're a racist, huh?"

"No, I'm not a racist. I just don't believe in that mixing stuff, because that is what I was taught growing up. I never looked at it any different."

"Let me ask you a question, Stella. When you bleed what color is it?"

"That's a silly question, red. The color of blood is red."

Peggy looked at me with a very serious look and began to tell me why she felt like my thinking was ignorant. "It's funny that you to say that, because I remember one day my daughter-in-law was cooking and accidentally cut herself – her blood was red too."

"That is because that's the color of blood. Did you think her blood would be another color?" I asked.

"Exactly!" She said not giving me a chance to respond. "When we bleed we all bleed the same color. You have been told the wrong thing and seeds of hate have been planted in your heart for years from nonsense of someone's opinion. Your parents taught you that, their parents taught them that mess, and so on and so on."

"See, I wasn't raised that way and I love every one of every color, regardless of their race. I feel if two people are happy together, then let them be. Their race shouldn't matter, and others should just let them be and leave them the heck alone. I wish you would try to look at things a little differently."

Mrs. Stella continued to tell Peggy about my mother and how they didn't have a relationship because she got married to a black man. She said all she could do was cry while telling her story. Peggy told her that the God who created the Universe loves them all and none different. Unfortunately, Mrs. Stella didn't have a clue as to who God was.

She said Peggy invited her to attend church services at the chapel at the nursing home, and she started going weekly. Mrs. Stella's friend Peggy talked to her about God and she used to be on drugs and He delivered her. Peggy told her she was not always the best mother. She had left her kids and was all over the place, but God saved her and turned her into a completely different woman. Mrs. Stella told me that Peggy formed a relationship with God about thirty years ago and her heart changed slowly, and she started to look at things in a different way.

"Carmen over time I watched Peggy and her family and how she loved on her daughter-in-law and grandchildren, and then I started to think about you and your sisters. A different feeling came into my heart. I couldn't help the tears that streamed down my face as I watched her love for them was so real. Watching them bothered me so much, it's like God started tugging on my heart to reach out to you."

After all of these years, finally I had my answer. "I am glad your heart changed, and you reached out."

I told her how I overheard Pretty Boy and my mother's conversation when I was younger, and his exact words were, "Mrs. Stella was prejudice and didn't love my mother because she married a black guy and had biracial children."

I also explained to her how I used to cry myself to sleep at night. I had been hurt for years and was praying for this day to come. "Again Carmen, I can't tell you how sorry I am. I love you and your sisters, and hope to meet my great granddaughters one day. I want to make the best of the days we have."

"I forgive you, but I have to wonder if everything is okay? Are you okay?"

"Yes baby, I'm fine. I just want to live every day the way God has intended.

A few weeks later Chasity and the girls started going with me to visit her, the day finally came when she met her great-granddaughters.

My life had done a complete three sixty and things had really taken off with *"Lovely Prosperous Ladies."* In fact, things were going so well that I no longer had to work at Mega Burgers & Fries. I could have stopped working earlier, but I guess I was a little afraid to step out on faith.

Natalie said, "Faith is the step when you hope for the best, but don't know what is going to happen."

If it wasn't for Natalie, *"Lovely Prosperous Ladies"* wouldn't exist today. I know it was only God who connected us. She was so full of life, and every time we spoke she had something positive to say. Natalie always said, "Remember

Philippians 4:13, *'I can do All things through Christ who strengthens me.'*

I may not have known many Scriptures by heart, but that was the one I did know. She told me to text it to myself and even considered wearing it on a shirt. I wouldn't have been surprised if she tried to get it wall papered in her house.

Once the website was up and running, Victoria told Alexis about my business and she called me back to Hot 106.9 to do another interview. The outcome of the opportunity to being able to promote my business on the radio was unbelievable. I also created social network accounts and the word about *"Lovely Prosperous Ladies"* quickly spread like wildfire.

God placed the people who were needed to help fulfill His Purpose in my life. They both believed in me even when I didn't believe in myself. "God didn't place ideas and gifts inside of us for us not to use them," was the constant voice of Natalie ringing in my ears. She made sure it was ingrained in my brain.

Natalie was such a beautiful person inside and out. She and I had spent a lot of time building the business and talking about our past. Her kid's father was released from prison a few months ago and had turned his life around. They were due to get married next year, and I couldn't be happier for her.

After talking to her I felt like I could do anything. I think everyone needs a Natalie in their life. Her answers were honest, whether I wanted to hear it or not. She said she wasn't a real friend if she couldn't be honest. She also told me I would learn and grow from certain situations.

Ultimately, we became business partners; she purchased Lovely Prosperous Ladies items and put it in her boutique to sell. I thanked God so much, because I know they were only doors that He could open. No man could have changed my life the way it had been changed within the last year and a half. So many organizations were purchasing items from "*Lovely Prosperous Ladies,*" that I had made $7,000, within the last month.

I loved my business so much that sometimes I couldn't sleep at night. I enjoyed meeting so many different women and hearing their stories. And to know that clothing I created was being worn by so many different women was amazing.

The feeling I received when someone posted their testimony on my website, or emailed me from around the country was worth more money than I could ever receive in life. Just a while ago I didn't know my purpose, was broke, living in poverty, and now I was living a life of purpose. However, the money could never amount to the lives that were being impacted.

I was invited to speak at a conference in New York, and it gave me an opportunity to set up as a vendor to put some of my products on display. I hadn't found anything to wear because I had been so busy. I had lost a total of seventy-five pounds since I moved back to Florida. I realized my weight wasn't only external, but it was more internal than anything.

Once I understood that concept and started to seek God, asking for help with my binges, my heart started to heal which caused the emotional eating to stop. I started eating right, and releasing the weight within was the outcome of me losing the physical weight. My mind, body, and soul were my focus because I knew it was imperative to my purpose. It was a hindrance at one time, but not anymore. Everyday my goal was to eat to live, and not live to eat.

I loved the way the dresses, skirts, and business suits fit my new curves. I wanted a different look with my change, so I thought it was time to put my curls to rest and wore my hair straight most of the time.

Chasity became my assistant and went with me to several events. She was very excited about New York and ecstatic to go to a place she had wanted to go to all of her life. I saw how "*Lovely Prosperous Ladies,*" inspired my sister. She even began to work on her dreams and goals. Now she believed if I could make my dreams come true, that she could do the same.

Overcoming The Battle

Chapter Twenty-Two

Thomas, was so interested in me and expressed how he wanted to get to know me better. Since the party we had been talking on the phone and even went out on a few dates. Thomas was such gentleman and a great dresser. It was definitely the first time I dated a guy of his stature. He was thirty-one years old with no kids and owned two businesses and a non-profit organization where he mentored misguided young men.

Thomas was a God-fearing man who had such a great vision for life. He loved God and put Him first in everything, which is what attracted me to him even more. After a few dates and long conversations over the phone we decided that we would work on being more than just friends. My actions towards him weren't always fair or friendly.

My actions towards Thomas also proved I wasn't ready to move onto another relationship. After my relationship with Devin I didn't want to trust, and feared trusting another man. It was obvious I hadn't completely healed from my past. I still held onto unforgiveness and bitterness in my heart. When you're in an abusive relationship for an extended period of time it could have a strong impact on your life. I had been so focused on helping other women; the main woman that needed to be delivered was me.

Thomas would open doors for me, never called me out of my name, and most of all he never ever put his hands on me or spoke to me in a disrespectful way. But even after all of that I still expected him to treat me the way Devin did. You know what they say, *"If it's too good to be true it usually is."* So, I believed it, but in this case, he was good. And because I was still hurt, not to mention I believed a lie that a man like Thomas couldn't love me and treat me as such, I couldn't receive him or his love. The man I prayed for was the very man I rejected.

Not being made whole, and continuing to walk around hurt will make you reject the very thing you desire. Hurt people hurt other people, and I had hurt Thomas with my actions. But I was grateful he didn't walk out of my life.

I started praying and talking to God, and He began to minister to me and showed me how I had to get to the root of my issue, and Devin wasn't the root, Pretty Boy was. I had carried and buried my hurt for many years and never dealt with it. I really had to pray and ask God to allow me to forgive him and take any bitterness or hate out of my heart.

Once I realized I had to release him, no longer would I be mad or upset he wasn't the father he should have been, or not even the fact that his apologies never seemed sincere. I was angry because he had hurt us and wasn't trying to become a better man, and that infuriated me. In order to put all of it behind me and move forward in my life, I had to deal to heal. No longer could I run away from the hurt of my father.

The girls and I were finally moving out of Smithstone James Apartments into our new place. We were able to find a really nice house across town in a great neighborhood with good schools. Thomas and some of his friends were nice enough to help us move. Although we were still renting, it felt great to get out of subsidized housing.

While the guys were moving the furniture, Pretty Boy entered the apartment. I knew this day was bound to come. I had to face him – there was no getting around it. "There goes my princesses, come give granddad a hug. I've missed y'all so much."

The twins had so much excitement in their voice, they missed him dearly. "Hey Granddad! Where have you been? You missed our party?"

"I know girls, I'm so sorry, but I was out of town for a while. I promise to make it up to you, do you forgive me?"

"Yaaahhh!" they said in unison.

I stood at the corner before entering the living room as I watched Pretty Boy kissing on their rosy cheeks. When he noticed me walk into the room he reached into his pocket and pulled out two ten dollar bills, handed the girls one each and told them to go play while he talked with me. The girls ran into their room as Thomas and his friends continued to move our items.

Thomas stuck his head in the door and asked me where to place a certain piece of furniture. Before I directed him, I introduced him to Pretty Boy. They shook hands and Thomas went back to his work. "Butterball, he seems like a really nice guy," he said with a hug.

For the first time I could embrace my father with forgiveness in my heart. One thing I said I would start trying to do was call him daddy. I thought I would give it a try, but

I guess deep down inside I couldn't because I didn't have the respect for him.

"Carmen, I'm so sorry. For all of these years I didn't see the person I was until recently. Oh, and Chasity gave me your address, I hope that's alright?"

"Yes, it's fine. And Daddy, I forgive you and I'm sorry. At the end of the day you are still my father. I hope you can forgive me?"

"Carmen, of course I forgive you, and you shouldn't be apologizing. It was because of my actions that you felt the way you did. I should have been a better man, I should have been a father, I am so sorry. God only knows if I could I would go back and make some changes. You know, God has been dealing with me on some things too?"

"Really?"

"Yes, He has. Butterball, I would like for us to start building a real daddy-daughter relationship. Where I'm not just calling you when I need something, but the kind of relationship where I call just to check on you. We can start going places together and the twins can come over on the weekends whenever you need a break."

Pretty Boy lowered his head as he continued. "Butterball, I don't know if it's too late, but I want to start being the father I haven't been for so many years. I want you to know I love you so much, you and your sisters."

"Yes Daddy, I would really like that."

Wiping the tears from his eyes, he lowered his head again, "I'm sorry I questioned you about Greg. I shouldn't have done that. I should have protected you."

"Daddy, you had no idea. I really do forgive you and I'm ready for us to start over with a clean slate."

"Well Butterball, I want you to know that Greg is facing twenty-five years to life and won't be able to hurt anyone else again. About six other little girls in his neighborhood came forth and filed charges, saying Greg had sexually violated them as well."

"I pray he sees what he has done and asks God to forgive him. I can't continue being mad and holding onto what he did to me for the rest of my life. That's not going to get me anywhere."

"I see your point baby, but enough about that. Your Grandma has been telling me all the things you've been doing with your business. She told me all about you traveling, and telling your story at conferences. I want you to know I think you are so brave and I'm very proud of you."

I couldn't help but smile because my dad was very sincere, and I knew he was proud of me. "Thanks, it's a lot of work, but it's all worth it in the end."

"And dang girl, you are looking good. I guess I got to drop the name "Butterball" huh?" He laughed.

"Thanks again, it's been a lot of work too! It's a daily process though."

"Well, Carmen, how much more do you have to move, I can help?"

"Oh, that would be great, the more help, the better. There isn't that much more left though."

"Can I take you and the girls to dinner after we finish."

"I would love that Daddy."

The Fatherless Daughter

I've never been so terrified to do something in my life. A little overwhelmed and "fear of the unknown" was trying to set in. I'm preparing to open my heart, and letting him in. The one I never trusted. Someone who has hurt me for so many years, and I don't think they even realize it.

I've been angry, bitter, and hurt years after years. I've cried so many tears! I've faked showing love for so long and now it's no more of that. I'm opening my heart to love, and love FOR REAL this time.

The man I expected to love me the most, a man I wanted to count on being there always. The man I've seen put himself before his own children. One of the reasons for having sex with different men was to fill this void of his missing love. Falling for men just like him, thinking they would love me, so therefore I no longer needed his.

For some reason, I continued to long for his love, and other men couldn't do it. Not realizing the disrespect, I was giving my body because I didn't have a care in the world. I found out later only God could replace everything I wanted to make my problem solver.

No longer will I hear the negative thoughts that run in my head to keep me in bondage of fear. The thoughts want to continue to feed the little girl within, but it's time for her to heal from what happened back then. I'm opening my heart with faith and God on my side being my guide. My dream came true, I genuinely could say "I love you daddy, and I know you love me too."

Signed: No longer a fatherless daughter

Chapter Twenty-three

Sometimes we think we've healed and released a situation until something happens that triggers it back to the surface. When it comes back to the surface we start to have those feelings we had before. The reality is we never moved on from it, we only buried it and walked around with those things being unresolved.

I thought I had released everything because I had forgiven Devin and had peace with our current situation. My relationship with my father was the root of most of my hurt, but I didn't know because I hid the feelings for years. The key was that I couldn't have complete peace until I went to the root of the hurt and got things right with him.

Many of our actions show how we really feel about situations despite what we're saying with our mouth. My actions showed I had a lot buried in my heart, but if anyone paid close attention by my actions, they may have known. When something is in someone's heart it will pour out through their actions, because out of our heart flows the issues of our life. We as people start to act out, respond, or receive certain behavior in life according to those issues. I had so much peace once I forgave my father.

Pretty Boy was calling every other day to check on us. We were going on movie and dinner dates regularly, sometimes more than once a week. He also has a family trip for us to go on a cruise planned in a few months. Even

Charlotte agreed to go. I truly loved him and enjoyed our daddy-daughter relationship.

I was seeing a different man from all of these years. Even though it was years later after he changed, the important part was that he changed. Before he changed I also had the peace wondering "what if he never changed." And I had peace with him not changing and still forgiving him. Some people may not get the closure or *I'm sorry* from ones that have hurt them, but everyone should still forgive and find the peace that they need for themselves if they don't receive the "*I'm sorry*" or a closure like mine and my father's. It is unfortunate every relationship won't turn out that way, but healing is still a must regardless of the outcome. Once I made peace with my father I was ready to continue a relationship with Thomas.

We had been in a celibate relationship for six months. Thomas wanted to give us another chance, which made me feel lucky because I hadn't treated him the best. I really enjoyed him as my friend, but loved it even more now that he was my man. Honestly, I did not know if I deserved a second chance, but Thomas said he wasn't giving up on us that quick, and each day he proved that to me.

Thomas loved working out, so we went on walks and worked out together, which helped me shed twenty-five more pounds. I loved how he was such a gentleman. He was always interested in where I wanted to go or what I wanted to do. Most of the time he had a bouquet of flowers in hand when he picked me up for our dates, or had flowers delivered, even though it wasn't a special occasion.

On one of our dates when I invited him over, I felt it necessary to let him know how much I appreciated him. "Thomas, I want you to know I'm so sorry about how I treated you before. I was a broken hurt little girl who didn't know how to receive your love."

"Carmen, that's the past. I just wanted you to see I'm different. I wanted you to see the Queen that you are and what you deserve, but now I understand, and I forgive you."

"I know you do, but I thought apologizing was something you also deserved. I should have told you about the relationship I was in before, the abuse, and all my other baggage. My kid's father told me no man like you would really love me, and I believed it."

"Well, I was patient, I let God guide me. He told me not give up on you. Now, if it was not for God, a brother would have been out!" He said smiling.

"Really?" I laughed.

"For real though, Carmen, I knew it was something different about you when I first laid eyes on you. Before you gave me a chance, I started praying for you. Not praying for you to give me a chance, but praying for the best for your life."

"Wow! I had no idea. Well, the prayers worked because you know when I met you I wasn't feeling you or anybody else for that matter."

"I know; I remember the look you gave me when I asked for your number."

"Was it that bad?"

"Uh yeah! I'm surprised a brother didn't get cut."

We both shared a laugh, which was one of the things I enjoyed about him. "It was cool though. Because when a man is guided by God, he is going to pursue and go after what is rightfully his."

"Oh, for real?"

"Yes, for real," he gave me a peck on the lips,

"Thomas, you can't be turning me on like that, and then expect for us not to have sex?"

"What I do?"

"Talking all sexy and about a man going after what's rightfully his, and then a peck on my lips. Baby, you don't think we can try it just a little."

"No ma'am, we cannot. I ain't playing with God like that. Carmen, I don't care how fine you are, and you are fine," he smiled. But... "It ain't going down!"

"Who's going to know, babe?"

Thomas looked up. "Did you really just ask me that? Okay, it's time for me to go, because I see you can't stop lusting after me right now," he said laughing.

"Okay, okay, I get it. I know the promise we made to God and ourselves."

"I'm glad you remember. Not until after marriage, you deserve that. More importantly, we agreed on God building our foundation His way."

"You're right baby. God knows I desire His will more than ours."

"Yep, and that's that, okay you ready to get this run on."

"As long as I am with you lover boy, I'm ready for anything."

"Okay, I'm glad you said that, because today we're doing six miles instead of four."

"Six? Naw, I can't do that."

"Yes, you can. Remember, we don't say can't. I got you, I promise."

"Let's go I guess."

"Don't be giving me that look, and that attitude either."

On our way out the door Thomas stopped me to assure me of his love. "Look, I love you, and I'm here for you and the twins. I promise you can count on me for anything. I believe you know that now, but I just wanted to tell you that."

"I do know that Thomas. I love you too. Only God could have sent you."

I had the biggest grin on my face as we continued out the door. I couldn't help but to thank God for the man he sent into my life, one that is so after His own heart. We both were very passionate about helping others and wanted to live our lives to the fullest intent of how God planned it.

Looking back on my relationship with Devin, I didn't realize God was holding someone so special for me. I thank God for second chances, because I almost missed out on a really great man. He didn't have to tell me twice I should be treated like a queen. Grandma made sure she drilled that in me the night at the hospital with Chasity. I was able to let go of my insecurities from thinking that Thomas was going to cheat or beat on me. Now I had peace I could trust him.

Occasionally, we double dated with Lloyd and Tamela when they were in town. Tamela and I had become close and started to communicate a lot. She supported *"Lovely Prosperous Ladies," and* wore (LPL) shirts when they went on tour, which caused more people to become interested.

The support was so overwhelming we received orders from people all over the country. It was more confirmation that God had placed this idea and vision in my heart. And because He gave it to me it was going to be a success, and HE would receive the glory for it. I thought *'Hey, God gave it to me, how could it not be a success?'*

What if I would have never done anything with the idea He put inside of me? I wouldn't know what it would have become. Now, I was willing to take a risk and step of faith, even if it looked like a possibility of failing. I wouldn't know if I would fail or if it would be a success if I never tried. I once heard someone say, "You could have a million dollar idea, but if you never do anything with it, you'll never see that million dollars." I believed that is so true.

Lloyd and Tamela were due to get married in two and a half months. They planned a wedding with a guest list of five hundred. The wedding party included thirty people because Tamela had a big family and couldn't leave anyone out. Lloyd's tour was doing great and most of his shows were sold out. I was amazed at how God had transformed him from an ex-drug dealer and ex-gang member to now a singing artist that was worth close to half a million dollars

Thomas and I were both in the wedding, so I had to make sure I didn't plan any events around their wedding date. Over a year ago I had made plans to get married and was so close to it, but here I was now supporting my friend who beat me to the punch. This is how life was supposed to be. Not catching your fiancé in the bed with some woman two weeks before your wedding.

Life was going great in Florida, but I did miss Texas, Charlotte, Aunt Isabel and Savannah. When Savannah heard me talk about Lloyd, she attended a show he performed at in Texas to meet him. Lloyd had gotten her V.I.P passes to get back stage and she had the opportunity to meet some of her favorite artists.

Savannah and I hadn't seen each other in almost a year, and I hadn't met my god-daughter Hope. There was an event I was invited to speak at in Houston, so I decided I would stay a few days to visit with my sister Charlotte, Savannah, and Aunt Isabel. The plan was to take the girls to visit their family. They would miss a few days from school, but I thought it would be okay since they had perfect attendance.

Savannah and I had a lot of catching up to do. My god-daughter Hope was so beautiful, and Savannah was in love. And, not with Theodore. "Oh, it's so good to see you! Savannah, Hope is gorgeous!"

"I miss you like crazy, friend. Yes, your god-daughter may be gorgeous, but she is keeping me busy."

"Okay, skip to it. Who is he?"

The smile on Savannah's face was one I had never seen before. "Don't laugh Carmen because he is different, and you know how I loved chocolate man, but I went a little outside of the box."

"What'chu mean girl, outside of the box?"

"Well, he ain't black Carmen," she said laughing.

"Hey, you are happy, and you've found love. Now, who is he?"

"His name is Chad; he is very successful and well known. His family owns a few farms."

"Chad Malone? No way!"

"Yeah girl we met on a blind date, my cousin Julia set up, you know him?"

"A blind date? Wow, what a small world. He came by the club a few times. And he left me the best tips ever. You know he was with a girl before that did him so wrong, but he is a great guy. Savannah, you have a good man, I'm super happy for you!"

"Yes, he is girl!!! Oh, my goodness, where do I begin about this amazing man. Thanks girl. I'm so in love with him. I didn't ever think I could meet a man like him."
"Well you deserve it."

I couldn't help but be excited for my friend because I knew she had a good man, and this time it was facts. I enjoyed my visit with her, but I had to leave to catch my flight back to Florida. I was so glad Savannah's life had turned around for the better. She and I both had wasted enough time on the wrong men.

Devin and I had started to form a relationship for our daughters' sake. Now when we spoke we weren't arguing all the time. He said things didn't work out with him and Tammy, but he was being a father to his son.

I had received a text from him one afternoon telling me he wanted to talk to me about something. I thought that was different, because he never texted me, only called to speak to the girls. As I picked up the phone and started to dial his number all kind of thoughts were going through my mind.

I wondered if he thought there was hope in getting me back, or if he wanted me to call to question me about Thomas and him being around his children.

Aunt Isabel told me he tried to ask her questions about him.

"Hello"

"Hi Devin, how are you?"

"I'm hanging in there. And you?"

"I'm amazing. Thanks for asking. What's up?"

"Carmen, I wanted to apologize to you for my selfish and immature ways. I ruined my family and I wanted to say I'm sorry and if you will forgive me."

"I forgive you Devin. And God knows I hope the best for your life."

"I realized how I was a little messed up because I treated Tammy the same way. But, I'm going to get better. I want to be a better person. I don't want my girls to have to experience a man like me, and end up paying for my bad karma."

"As long as you're the father you need to be for the girls, and you're their first love and example of how a man should treat a woman, they should be alright. You still have a chance at getting better at that."

"Yeah, you right. But I don't want or need a woman right now. I need to focus on me and my children. Hey, I called to see about getting some help to start some counseling."

"Devin, that is awesome! I went through some counseling, still going to counseling. It was one of the best decisions I could have made. God wouldn't put these tools here if they weren't needed."

"True. Carmen, I'm proud of you, and the woman you have become. I know you're not the same woman I was with before. I see what God has done in your life and what He's doing through you."

"Thanks Devin, I appreciate that."

"I want a relationship with God, but I don't know if he wants me. He will have a lot on his plate dealing with me."

"God wants to receive everyone Devin."

"I started going to church."

"Really! Devin that is amazing!"

"Yeah, I decided to give it another chance. I don't make it every Sunday, but I try."

"It's a process, just keep going and receiving, you will see the change."

"Carmen, I have had thoughts and I've been thinking of giving my life back to Christ."

I couldn't believe it; I knew only God was in the midst. And I had to take the opportunity that was at hand. "Devin, would you like to do something?"

"Do what?"

"What if we said The Prayer of Salvation right here, right now? You don't have to wait until you go back to church to give your life to God, you can do it now."

"Carmen, I don't know, I can't guarantee I'm going to stop everything today."

"Devin, it's not about that, it is about you repenting, making up in your mind to allow Christ to come into your life, guide you, and make the change, it's one day at a time. And God knows that."

"I know I'm tired of feeling empty inside, doing all this useless stuff to fill this void."

"You can do it Devin, but you must trust God. See, God wants you to take His hand, so He can show you the plan He has for your life."

Devin took a deep breath and waited about twenty seconds before he started to speak. "Okay Carmen, I will do it."

I was smiling from ear to ear. Even though Devin and I were no longer together, I was glad for the change he was making in his life, and very proud of him for taking this step. "Great! Just repeat after me."

Devin repeated the Prayer of Salvation asking God to forgive him of his sins and to show him a different way. I encouraged him to read and meditate on a Scripture to help him with his daily walk with God. Proverbs 16:9 *"A man's mind plans his way, but the Lord directs his steps and makes them sure."*

Chapter Twenty-four

As I was sitting at my desk working on different projects for *Lovely Prosperous Ladies* my phone rang, and an unknown number flashed across the Caller ID. Tears instantly rolled down my face. Chasity continued to ask what was wrong, but I couldn't respond right away. It was the nursing home calling to deliver news I never imagined to receive.

Mrs. Stella had a heart attack and died. It was unexpected, because she had just received a good report from her doctor's visit only three weeks ago. Chasity and I were glad we were able to build a relationship with her while we had the chance. Charlotte said she wished she would have been able to meet her.

About three weeks after Mrs. Stella passed I received a phone call for my sisters and me to meet with a judge and the Executor of Estate for Mrs. Stella's estate. He said we were to be present during the reading of Mrs. Stella's Will. I had no idea she had an estate and never knew we were in a will, we had only built a relationship with her within the past year.

When Chasity and I arrived at the court house for the reading we were surprised to see Charlotte was already there. "Hey Charlotte, when did you get in town?"

"I just landed about an hour ago, I didn't know if I would be able to make it since it was last minute. Then I said I wasn't going to miss out on my cut," she laughed, rubbing her index and thumb finger together.

"Charlotte stop; you don't even know if this has anything to do with receiving any money."

We were so caught up in our conversation we didn't notice the look on the Executor of Estate's face. He was impatiently waiting for us to finish so he could start. "Hello, my name is Jeffery Hall, I'm the Executor of Estate and I will be reading Mrs. Carson's Will today, and may I ask who you are."

I reached my hand out giving him a hand shake. "I'm Carmen Wilson, you spoke with me on the phone, and these are my sisters Charlotte and Chasity Wilson."

"Nice to meet all of you – please have a seat so we can begin, this shouldn't take long."

As we took our seats Mr. Hall pulled Mrs. Stella's Will out of his briefcase and didn't waste any time as he went right to reading the Will. "In the reading of the Will for the deceased Elizabeth "Stella" Carson, the following should be dispersed as?"

He paused for a moment before he continued and all I could think of was WOW! Dispersed? Was that correct? To my sisters and me? "The estate is in the amount of $500,000.00 and $250,000.00 of that portion is to be dispersed to Carmen Wilson, $125,000.00 goes to Charlotte Wilson and the remaining $125,000.00 goes to Chasity Wilson."

"What?!" I asked flabbergasted.

"We are rich, that's what!" Charlotte said with a big smile on her face.

"Sir, our grandmother left us this money? Are you sure?" Chasity asked.

Mr. Hall looked at us with a frown on his face before he responded sarcastically. "I would not have read this information if it wasn't in the Will. My job is to read the Will and make sure the estate is dispersed the way it is written."

"Sir, even though she was our grandmother, we are just shocked, because we only formed a relationship with her a year ago. Can I ask when this will was created?"

"Carmen, you are doing too much. You are asking all of these crazy questions. He gonna end up saying it was a mistake," Charlotte said cutting her eyes.

"No ma'am there is not a mistake at all, the Will is correct," Mr. Hall said shaking his head.

"Carry on Carmen, ask all you want then," Charlotte laughed.

"Where did she get this money from?" I asked very curious.

"Why can't you girls just take the estate how I read it. Your checks are already cut and ready to go," he said irritated that I was still asking questions.

"We thought she was poor. We didn't know she had any money, and we're curious," Chasity said.

Mr. Hall took a deep sigh before he explained

"Well, let's see – it looks like her great grandparents owned slave plantations in Georgia, North Carolina, and

South Carolina. They left it to your grandmother and she sold the land about six months ago, putting the funds in an Estate when she made out her will."

My sisters and I stared in amazement and couldn't believe what we were hearing. The irony in the fact that our grandmother at one point was prejudice, did not believe in blacks and whites dating because her family told her it wasn't right, had left us half of a million dollars was mind blowing to us. Only to find out that our family owned slave plantations. Now our grandmother had sold the land and put it in an Estate for her biracial grandchildren to have once she passed. *'Wouldn't her great grandfathers that left the land that was passed down to her be very disappointed,'* I thought.

After he passed out our checks, we sat for a moment before we could leave, besides Charlotte. She probably was already in line at the bank to cash her check before Chasity and I left. This was a blessing and a miracle. I already knew what I was going to do with my portion. It may have looked impossible, but I trust God and know with Him ALL THINGS ARE POSSIBLE!

Trust Him

Don't look to the back or to the side, just look straight
ahead and stay focused on God.
Even though we may not know what is next to come, God
will always know what's around the corner.
At times we may be in the zone, feeling all along, but trust
and believe, God was there all along.
If you're feeling stressed and for days you cry, remember
God said," For you, I will get on the cross and die."
"I love you so much, and I'm no man, therefore, I shall not
tell a lie."
He is your heavenly father, a healer, a comforter, and when
it seems like your ends won't meet, he will come through.
He is your provider…YES, He is Jehovah -Jireh.
Now as His child He wants you to cast the cares of the
world on Him.
His love for you is unbelievable, and with
HIM..ANYTHING IS ACHIEVABLE!
You can do ALL things through Christ who strengthens
you.
Despite the words of what doubters may say, God says,
"Take my hand, watch and see, you will be amazed by me.
The accomplishment of the mission, because it is "I who
has given you the vision. God says, "With me and you,
there is NOTHING that I can't DO!"

Overcoming The Battle

Chapter Twenty-five
A Year Later

Thomas and I had been married for three months and we couldn't have been happier. He surprised me by proposing at Lloyd's and Tamela's wedding reception. We had our home built while we were engaged. It was a beautiful brick, four bed-room two-story house with a two-car garage. The girls loved their home, especially since they had their own rooms decorated with their favorite cartoon characters.

Thomas and I were so glad we waited until we were married before we had sex. We were both very excited to make love and spent a lot of our time in the room while we were on our honeymoon. We have only been married for three months, and let's just say, we have been very busy.

We found out last week that I was almost three months pregnant. We conceived our child the night of our honeymoon or sometime afterwards. Both of us were very excited, but I believe Thomas was a little more excited that he was going to be a father. There wasn't a preference of rather we wanted a boy or a girl, we only desired to have a healthy baby.

"Carmen I'm so proud of you, going after everything God has promised you. I mean you inspire me, and I couldn't have been blessed with a better wife, but I do have a request?"

"Yes, my love?"

Before he mentioned his request, he bent down placing his hand on my stomach and kissed it a few times before coming back up to kiss me on my lips.

"Well baby, you have been doing a lot of traveling, Canada, London, and Africa, that's amazing and again I'm very proud of you. But when your six months I would like for you not to be doing so much traveling and just focus on the baby."

"Thomas?"

"I know you love what you do and were purposed for it, but you still have three more months left, come on baby?"

As hard as it was for me to agree to what he was asking, I tried my best to reason and see his point. One thing he was right about for sure was I loved what I did, with all my heart.

"Ok, babe. I get your point; I will do it. I will see if Chasity can go on my behalf if any traveling events come up."

"Yes! Thank you, Thank you!"

"Your Welcome."

I said rolling my eyes but also smiling

"You want regret it, I have so much planned for you to receive the Queen treatment you deserve."

"Oh, really huh?"

"Yes really! Now can we go eat wife?"

"You don't have to tell me twice; I'm right behind you husband!"

Lovely Prosperous Ladies organization had officially gone worldwide and was making an impact on others in different countries. With the money Mrs. Stella left, I gave $50,000.00 to my grandma to put towards her purchasing a bigger and newer home, and the remaining $200,000.00, I found two buildings and turned them into Enrichment Centers. One in Tampa, Florida and the other one in Houston, Texas. The center in Tampa was run by me, Victoria, Chasity, Grandmother and some other women from Tampa. The Houston center was being operated by Aunt Isabel, Charlotte, Savannah and some other women in the Houston area.

The centers were safe havens for women who had been raped, in abusive relationships, single mothers and their kids who were homeless. There was a waterfall fountain in the middle of the floor in each center, which represented cleansing. We asked the women, when they came into the centers if they would put their hands under the waterfall which was symbolic of them being cleansed from their battles and adversity they had experienced. It was a representation that they would defeat their battle and their battle wouldn't defeat them.

I dedicated the centers to my mother and Mrs. Stella. If it wasn't for her, the centers wouldn't have been in existence. The enrichment centers also had counselors that provided counseling. Savannah's mother visited the center one day, and from that day their relationship started to turn around. She and her mother were taking counseling classes together. They now had a mother-daughter relationship they never had before.

I sat back and looked over my life and words couldn't express how I felt about how God had turned my life around. If there was one word to say how I felt, it would be indescribable, and I could only give God all of the Glory. If it weren't for God, my life would not be what it is today.

I was interviewed a few months ago in London by a very popular magazine that sold all over the world. I must admit, even though I had spoken in front of thousands of people I was a little nervous. I couldn't help but think of how I would be exposed to millions, maybe even billions of people by them reading this interview.

"Thank you again Carmen for allowing us to share your testimony to the world by publishing it in our magazine. This won't take too long."

"Your very welcome, and this is such an honor. Thank you, Bernice, so much for the opportunity.

"Let's move right along with the first question."

"What led you to the idea of starting Lovely Prosperous Ladies?"

"I had met a few women, along with myself who had encountered obstacles as molestation, rape, domestic violence, and other obstacles. I saw how because of these obstacles some women didn't have a voice, and struggled with their identity. I wanted to be bold and be that voice to inspire women to not allow their adversity to overcome them, but to change their perspective and for their adversity to be the motivation that pushes them into their destiny."

"That's powerful Carmen and so true. Sometimes, in the midst of when things are happening we can't see God's plan or that it will really work out for our good like Romans 8 says."

"Exactly!"

"Did you ever imagine the organization spreading all over the world and becoming worldwide?"

"I had no idea what the outcome would be to be honest, but no I didn't. I realized the more I said, "yes to God" the more I said, "I surrender God, allow your will to be done and not my own," I continued to see the unbelievable, and more than I could ever imagine that could happen in my own power.

God gets the Glory for this outcome. Because sometimes I didn't understand how it would happen as God guided me and knew I had to trust God completely. It took operating in faith and saying no to fear.

"Where do you see Lovely Prosperous Ladies in years to come?"

"I see Lovely Prosperous Ladies being an organization I hoped to never end. One which will be passed down to my daughters, passed down to their daughters, and generations of generations to come."

"That's Awesome Carmen! And I definitely believe that will happen."

"Thank you, Bernice, I believe it too."

"What advice do you have for someone who has battled with their identity, someone struggling to discover who they are, what would you tell them Carmen?"

"The advice I would have for them would be that, "I would tell them their identity is in Christ. And they must seek God to discover that identity. I would tell them what my friend Lloyd told me, "The Creator knows all of the instructions to its product that it created. God knows everything about you inside and out, so seek Him so He can tell you who you are. Also, not too focus on what others think or say. People didn't design you, therefore they can't define you, only God can do that."

"Anything else to go along with that?"

"Also, whatever their dreams or goals are in life they must believe it will be their own faith that will make it come true, regardless of what anybody else thinks.

"I would also encourage them that everything negative ever said about them is not true. They shouldn't let their history determine who they can become. Once God started placing the right people into my life to empower me, it woke something up inside of me every time they spoke."

"Afterwards, I had to believe that what I saw happen for others could also happen for me. So, I took a step out of my comfort zone to do something I believed would work, despite what others thought. More importantly, what God led me to do. I started to believe the unbelievable, and the unbelievable started to happen."

Mark 9:23 says, *"Jesus said to him, that if anyone can believe, all things are possible to him that believes."*

"Well that concludes our interview Carmen, again, thanks so much for your time. And have a safe trip back to the states."

"Again, it has been a pleasure Bernice, I sure will, I'm excited to get back home to my family."

I couldn't believe almost four years ago that I was confused about who I was, and what my purpose was in life. I no longer have to ask who I am? My name is Carmen Wilson-Morris, I'm a wife, a mother, and I am the CEO and Founder of *Lovely Prosperous Ladies*, and a motivational speaker.

I AM AN OVERCOMER!!!

Overcoming The Battle

Made in the USA
Columbia, SC
03 March 2019